The m[illegible] with his elbow. He darted an anxious glance around the schoolyard. Had anyone seen him? Desperately eager to be rid of the body, he dumped it quickly inside. Suddenly he heard the crunch of a foot on gravel. He slammed the trunk shut and darted back underneath the stairs. From there he watched Laurie Wentworth jog past his car, her ponytail swinging. She glanced at the car but ran on by.

The murderer took out his keys and went around to the back of the car to lock it. It was then that he saw the thin fabric hanging out of the trunk. Her skirt! The dead girl had worn a long, sheer skirt. In his haste to slam the trunk shut, he had not made sure the skirt was tucked inside. Now the flimsy material fluttered in the breeze, advertising the dead body. Laurie must have seen it. That was probably why she had looked at his car. She might remember it later and put two and two together. She would be able to identify the car. Suddenly he knew he was going to have to get rid of her. No problem. He exhaled slowly. In fact, it would be a pleasure.

Read these terrifying thrillers
from HarperPaperbacks!

Babysitter's Nightmare
Sweet Dreams
Sweetheart
Teen Idol
*Running Scared**
by Kate Daniel

And look for

Class Trip
by Bebe Faas Rice

The Nightmare Inn series
#1 *Nightmare Inn*
#2 *Room 13*
#3 *The Pool**
by T. S. Rue

* coming soon

Dead Girls Can't Scream

Janice Harrell

HarperPaperbacks
A Division of HarperCollins*Publishers*

This is a work of fiction. The characters, incidents, and dialogues are products of the author's imagination and are not to be construed as real. Any resemblance to actual events or persons, living or dead, is entirely coincidental.

HarperPaperbacks *A Division of* HarperCollins*Publishers*
10 East 53rd Street, New York, N.Y. 10022

Produced by Daniel Weiss Associates, Inc., 33 West 17th Street, New York, New York 10011.

First printing: June, 1993

Printed in the United States of America

HarperPaperbacks and colophon are trademarks of HarperCollins*Publishers*

10 9 8 7 6 5 4 3 2 1

Dead Girls Can't Scream

Chapter One

"How does it feel when you have a psychic fit?" Katie Sloan asked her best friend as they skipped down the stairs.

"Pu-leeze!" Nicole Devereaux tucked a stray blond hair back into her French braid. "I wouldn't exactly call them 'fits.' I just get this cold feeling . . . and then it's like I know things I shouldn't. Things I can't see, things that haven't even happened yet. I can see beyond the ordinary, the mundane."

"Oh." Katie looked unconvinced.

"I guess I have something that other people don't have. You might call it a special sensitivity."

The murderer could hear the soles of the girls' shoes grating on the metal staircase above his head. He was careful to keep to the dark shadows under the stairs; he did not move an inch. He was even afraid to breathe. The staircase ran from the top level of A wing to the open path alongside the school. When the girls reached the ground, they turned toward the front of A wing without a glance in his direction.

"So you're telling me you knew Mrs. Ennis was going to make us take that pop test?" Katie asked.

"Yup. I had a feeling about it."

"And you didn't even tell me?"

"I wasn't sure," said Nicole. "It was more of a psychic twinge. But if something big were going to happen, I think I could tell for sure. A pop test just doesn't register much spiritually."

The murderer breathed a sigh of relief as the girls moved farther away and their voices faded. In a moment they had turned the corner of the building and disappeared from view. The coast looked clear, but still he felt nervous. He almost hadn't heard them coming. If they had come down the stairs just two minutes later, it would have been all over for him. They had no business back here, he thought resentfully. Most people used the front staircase of A wing. At four o'clock, he should have had the place to himself. Everyone had gone home except for the jocks and the band members, and they were way over in the fields past the gym.

He would have preferred to wait until dark, but he knew it might be more dangerous to move the body at night than during the late afternoon. The police patrolled the school grounds after dark, keeping an eye out for possible vandalism. His lone car parked on the service drive would have been all too obvious, whereas right now it was fairly inconspicuous. No one was supposed to park there, but teachers did it all the time and so did students carrying special projects back and forth from the classrooms.

His breath was coming in ragged gulps, and he had to stand quietly for a moment until he calmed down. Then he bent to pick up the body. The dead girl was covered by a rough wool blanket, and he did not want to uncover her, so he groped clumsily under the blanket to find his grip. He slipped one hand under her neck and the other under her knees. He felt the strain in the back of his legs as he struggled to a half-standing position with the body in his arms. In life she had been a small girl who had probably weighed no more than a hundred pounds. He was surprised at how heavy she seemed now that she was dead.

His pulse pounded in his throat as if it might

choke him, but he forced himself to move slowly and steadily. It took only a few seconds to carry the body to his car, where he'd left the trunk unlocked and slightly ajar. When he nudged the trunk with his elbow, it suddenly flew wide open. He darted an anxious glance around the schoolyard. Had anyone seen him?

Desperately eager to be rid of the body, he quickly dumped it inside. The blanket caught on the trunk latch and was pulled away from the dead girl's face. He stared a moment at her slack mouth, her disheveled hair, and her vacant blue eyes. He should have closed the eyes, he thought, and put pennies on them. Wasn't that what they did to keep the murdered person's ghost from walking? As he reached to pull the blanket back over her face, he heard the crunch of a foot on gravel. He slammed the trunk shut and darted back underneath the stairs. From there he watched a blond girl in sweat pants jog past his car, her ponytail swinging. She glanced at the car but ran on by. It was Laurie Wentworth, from the track team.

He stood in the shadows for several minutes after she had passed, his heart thudding so loudly he was sure she could hear it. But he heard nothing. She was not coming back for a second look. He was safe. Even if Laurie came back, she would see nothing. The body was hidden in his trunk.

He took out his keys and went around to the back of the car to lock it. The last thing he wanted to risk was the trunk popping open and displaying its grisly contents while he was driving. It was then that he saw the thin fabric fluttering in the breeze. Her skirt! The dead girl had worn a long, sheer skirt made of a filmy green and blue material. In his haste to slam the trunk shut, he had not made sure the skirt was tucked inside. A good-sized swath of the material had been caught when he closed it. Now the flimsy material fluttered in the breeze, advertising the dead body.

With trembling fingers, he opened the trunk and stuffed the scrap of material back in. A minute later, he was in the car, backing onto the service drive. Laurie must have seen the bit of skirt fluttering there. That was probably why she had looked at his car. But she had kept running because what she saw meant nothing to her. The problem was that she might remember it later and put two and two together. She would be able to identify the car. Suddenly he knew he was going to have to get rid of her. No problem. He exhaled slowly, his hands tightening on the steering wheel. In fact, it would be a pleasure.

Chapter Two

Katie ran her fingers restlessly through her short dark hair. It was seven fifteen and play rehearsal still hadn't begun. She glanced at her watch and wondered if Mr. Panovitch, the drama teacher, was going to keep them late. That wouldn't be fair since it was his fault they hadn't begun on time. Neither he nor Millicent Crenshaw, who had the lead, had arrived yet.

"We could play tic-tac-toe," Katie's boyfriend, Steve Patton, suggested. "Or would you rather make out?"

"Here?" Katie blushed.

"Just kidding." He lifted her hand to his lips and began to nibble gently on her fingers.

"That tickles." Katie giggled. "Besides, you're supposed to kiss a lady's hand, not eat it."

"But you taste so good!" He flashed her a brilliant smile.

Katie hadn't been able to believe her luck when Steve moved to town. Since ninth grade she had dreamed that some fascinating new boy would show up and fall in love with her, but all the new boys had been either nerdy types who were deeply interested in computers or jocks who were practically subhuman. Steve, with his long legs and quicksilver smile, was different. There was a mixture of sadness and suppressed excitement in him that reminded Katie of a steamy romance novel. Not to mention that he looked good. She loved his teddy-bear-brown eyes and his low, sexy voice. When he had joined the drama club and started asking her out, she'd considered it proof that dreams could come true.

"I've got half a mind to drop out of drama," grumbled Rage Michaels, a pale, skinny boy in black leather pants. "Who needs this?"

"Oh, come on," said Nicole. "Just because you didn't get the part you wanted is no reason to be that way. I'm only in the chorus, and you don't see me complaining. In fact, I think it's more fun if you don't have a zillion lines to memorize."

Until Steve moved to town, Rage had always been the drama star. But since this fall's production was a musical, Rage's thin singing voice had lost him the lead. Katie glanced around. She was sure that all over the auditorium the talk was pretty much the same. Kids were gossiping about Mr. Panovitch's weirdness and complaining about how the parts had been distributed. Some things never changed.

"I wonder where Millicent is," Steve said. "It's not like her to be late like this."

Katie felt a flutter of uneasiness. She was sure Steve had never noticed what Millicent was like before they had begun rehearsing the play.

Katie had hoped to get the lead herself, but as soon as she had heard Millicent sing, she had known it was no contest—Millicent was great. Although she was a slight, insignificant-looking girl, she had the vibrant singing voice that was perfect for musical comedy.

"Maybe she's figured out that Mr. P.'s always late," Katie said lightly, "and she's timed it so she'll slide in at just the same time he does."

Katie realized she was feeling jealous already and Millicent hadn't even arrived yet. It was impossible for her to get used to seeing Steve put his arms around Millicent in the play, even though she knew they were only acting.

A tall boy in ripped jeans scrambled up on the stage. "Since you're all here . . ." Mike Green raised one hand and soberly looked at them. His hair was growing out from when his head was shaved, and its short, bristled appearance made him look perpetually surprised. "I suggest we have vespers," he said. "Let us bow our heads."

"Boo!" came cries from all over the auditorium.

"Somebody give me a rotten tomato," Nicole yelled.

"I'm going to get something to drink," Rage said. "We'll probably be here all night." Looking disgusted, he stalked out.

"Drama people!" Katie said. "Why do they have to be so weird? Like when Mike stood on the table in the cafeteria the other day and said, 'Yes, I *will* kiss you for a dollar.'"

"Scared me to death," Steve agreed. "I was afraid he was talking to me."

"Mike is a typical drama person," Katie said. "And look at Rage. Why can't we call him Ralph anymore? It's his name."

"Come on, Katie. Would you want people to call you Ralph?" Steve asked lightly.

"I think he's dieting. He gets skinnier every day. I guess he's hoping he'll get cheekbones. Ever since he saw that Doors movie, he's been trying to look like Jim Morrison."

"He's got a long way to go," Steve said, grinning. "But at least he doesn't go around claiming he's psychic like Nicole does."

"Yeah, but for all we know Nicole may *be* psychic."

"Hah!"

"It's possible," Katie insisted loyally.

"Okay, I'll stop making fun of Nicole if you stop dumping on Rage. After all, he was the one who talked me into doing drama. 'Great cast parties,' he said, 'and pretty girls,' and I already see he was right about the girls." He grinned. "Let me have those fingers back. I missed lunch."

"You're breaking my heart." Katie tucked her fingers under her arms.

Katie had been surprised to learn that Rage and Steve knew each other before Steve moved to town. Rage's father lived in Steve's old hometown and the boys had played together when Rage went to visit. Katie thought it was strange that they were friends—their personalities were so different—but she knew that boys' friendships were not at all like girls'. When boys said they were friends, it often only meant that they hung out together, not that they discussed their feelings, like girls did. Steve and Rage had been friends for years, but Katie was sure neither of them ever knew what the other was really thinking.

She wondered about Steve's life before he'd

come to Rock Creek. She had always lived in the same town and the same neighborhood, and she imagined it would be awful to have to pick up and move away. But if moving had been tough on Steve, he kept it to himself. When she asked him about his old town, he always said talking about himself was boring or cracked a joke. Was he homesick? Did he miss his old friends? What was he thinking?

But right now, Katie admitted to herself, she was not too eager to know what was on Steve's mind. She was afraid he was thinking about Millicent. She decided to test him. "Speaking of eccentric, how about those safety-pin earrings Millicent wears all the time?" Katie shot Steve an anxious look.

"I like them," said Steve.

Katie winced.

"I guess I've gotten used to them," Steve went on. "They look all right to me." He threw his arm around Katie and smiled. "Face it, you're not going to find the straightest bunch of kids doing drama."

"You're right. Except for thee and me, nobody around here's really straight. Maybe we're the ones who are weird."

"Good evening, people!" Mr. Panovitch's voice boomed from the back of the auditorium. "I hope you are all prepared to be brilliant." The drama coach strode toward the stage, rubbing his hands together. He was a small, plump man with an air of self-importance. "To your places, children. It's time to work, work, work."

"Millicent's not here yet," Nicole told him.

"What do you *mean* she's not here?" Mr. Panovitch cried. "It's twenty minutes after seven. There is no excuse for this, none at all. Only the most pressing business kept me this late myself." He blew out his breath in a quick puff that made his plump cheeks vibrate. "We will not wait any longer. The show must go on. Katie, stand in for Millicent and we will begin at once. To your places! As for Millicent, this is the kind of behavior I cannot put up with! We do not attend rehearsal any old time we please, my dear people. We attend rehearsal without fail and on time!" He clapped his hands. "Hurry, hurry, boys and girls. Believe me," he added in a different voice, "Millicent had better have a good excuse. I mean, the girl had better be dead."

Katie and Steve trudged up the steps to the stage. The cast began walking through the play, not bothering with the fine points of emoting, but concentrating more on being sure everyone was in the right place and that people weren't bumping into one another. Katie was surprised to discover that she knew most of Millicent's lines already. Perhaps that was because she had so often imagined herself in the part. But when they came to the part of the play where she was to kiss Steve, she couldn't remember what to say. Mr. Panovitch fed her the line. "But what is a kiss?" she repeated after him in her best piping leprechaun voice. "Is it as good as ice cream?"

"Better. Let me give you one." Steve gave her a private wink and swept her into his arms for a long kiss.

"No need for so much feeling, Steve," Mr. Panovitch said dryly as the kids laughed.

When the cast took a break at eight, there was still no sign of Millicent. Katie felt a guilty tremor of pleasure. She had been secretly hoping something awful would happen to Millicent. Now she began to worry that maybe it had. As far back as she could remember, Millicent had never missed a rehearsal before. Why hadn't she shown up?

Nicole tugged at Katie's sleeve. "Why don't you call Millicent's house and find out why she's not here?"

"Why me?" asked Katie. "I don't even know Millicent that well."

"You know her better than I do. I think you ought to give her a call. Just to check on her."

Katie started to protest, but suddenly she realized that Nicole looked uncomfortable.

"You're having a funny feeling about Millicent, aren't you, Nic?" Katie asked sharply.

"I just wish you'd call her," Nicole said stubbornly.

Katie didn't answer. Now thoroughly alarmed, she slipped away to the lobby and dialed the Crenshaws' number. She had to keep telling herself that Millicent wouldn't have had a fatal car accident just because Katie wanted her part in the play. Wishes couldn't hurt anyone.

The phone rang a few times before Mrs. Crenshaw answered it.

"Hello?"

"Uh, Mrs. Crenshaw? This is Katie Sloan. You don't know me, but I'm in the drama club with Millicent. We were sort of wondering why she didn't show up for rehearsal tonight. She isn't sick or anything, is she?"

"She's not there? I don't understand it. She was going to have a quick hamburger, do her homework at the library, and then go straight to rehearsal. Are you sure she's not there?"

"Yes," Katie said. "Maybe she got a flat tire or something."

"It seems so strange," muttered Mrs. Crenshaw. "George, this is a friend of Millicent's. She says Millicent hasn't shown up at rehearsal."

Katie spoke to the Crenshaws for a few more minutes, but none of them could figure out where Millicent might be. She hoped she hadn't made a mistake in calling the Crenshaws' house. What if Millicent was in the library making out with some new boyfriend? She would not thank Katie for calling attention to her absence.

Katie went back into the auditorium and slipped into the seat next to Steve. "I just called Millicent's house. Her parents don't know where she is."

"She must have forgotten, that's all."

"I suppose so."

The dead body lay in the trunk of the car until two A.M. The murderer reflected that he hadn't needed to set his alarm clock—he couldn't sleep anyway. He was keyed up with a high that wouldn't go away, a pleasurable blend of excitement and fear. He knew one wrong step could destroy him. But he was sure he would not make a wrong step.

He backed his car out of the driveway and drove without lights until he was far from his neighborhood. Only a few cars were on the main road at that hour, and none of them knew his secret. He smiled when he thought of how people would react if they knew he had a dead girl in his trunk.

The city's landfill was on an isolated stretch of road past town. He had expected it to be a pit of some kind with old tires and junk littered about. Instead it was several bulldozed acres of dirt. Even in the dim light it looked like the wasteland it was, colorless in the moonlight, with bits of tire and board sticking up through the smooth dirt. Slowly, he backed his car up to the edge of the leveled dirt and stopped. He wasn't sure how solid the fill was. His wheels might get stuck or, worse, his tires might pick up a nail. But it didn't matter that he couldn't pull in closer. He was close enough. He got out and unlocked the trunk, taking a quick, cautious look around as he turned the key. Out on the main road a truck sped by, making a high whistling sound.

It was harder to get the body out of the trunk than it had been to dump it in, and he grunted with the effort. As he lifted her, he was careful not to let the blanket slip off. He only had to carry her a few feet before laying her down under one of the bushes that rimmed the landfill. He then uncovered her, folded the blanket, and put it back in his trunk. He had only one thing left to do.

A few seconds later, a flash lit up the body where it lay by the bush. Afterward, he let his camera dangle carelessly from its strap and grimaced at the body.

Dead girls were ugly, he thought.

He turned away, got back in his car, and drove slowly away from the landfill.

He glanced back at the fill as he pulled out on the main road. He was glad to see that the body wasn't visible from the road. Bodies were surprisingly easy to dispose of. Getting rid of her car had been the hard part. That afternoon, he had had to drive it from the school parking lot to the mall. Then he had walked four miles back to the school, being careful not to go along any main thoroughfare where he might be recognized. Once there he had retrieved his own car.

Now no one could connect Millicent's murder with the school or with him. Everyone would assume some drifter had killed her. Except Laurie Wentworth. He had almost forgotten her. The stupid girl who had been jogging. Laurie might make the connection. But he would soon take care of her.

Chapter Three

"Did you hear?" Nicole's face was white. "They found Millicent's body at the dump! She was strangled!"

"I can't believe it," said Tracy Higgins, a short, plump girl with pale-lashed blue eyes. "She was sitting right next to me in Spanish yesterday!"

"She must have been kidnapped," Nicole said. "They found her car at the mall. It wasn't locked, and the keys were still in it."

"I always lock my car," Tracy put in breathlessly. "And I park right under those big lights if I have to go to the mall at night. I never park next to a van, either. You never can tell who might be hiding inside a van."

"It could have happened to you or me!"

Nicole shuddered. "Well, I don't know about you, but I'm not going to the mall until they catch him," said Tracy.

"Use your brain, Tracy," hissed Nicole. "He could be anywhere by now."

The two girls unconsciously edged toward the sunny verge of the passageway behind the auditorium.

"Well, nobody would kidnap me!" Tracy insisted. "I don't care what they did, whether they had a gun or a knife or what, I'd just say 'kill me right here if you want to, but I'm not going anywhere.'"

"Give me a break, Tracy. You don't know what you'd do if it came down to it." Nicole spotted Katie walking toward them from the administration building. "Katie!" she cried. "Did you hear about Millicent?"

Katie hurried over to them.

"She was murdered!" Nicole said hoarsely. "They found her body this morning!"

Katie's face became pale. "I knew something must be wrong when she didn't show up at rehearsal." She huddled herself more tightly in her wool jacket, looking as though she might pass out.

"It turns out she didn't come home last night, so her parents called the police. They found her car at the mall. The keys were in it and there was no sign of a struggle or anything. She was just gone! Then, this morning, a man driving a garbage truck found her body at the landfill."

"I'll bet she didn't lock her car," Tracy put in smugly. "I *always* lock my car. He was probably hiding inside it waiting for her."

"But what was she doing at the mall anyway when she was supposed to be at rehearsal?" Katie asked.

"She must have gone by there before rehearsal and that's when he got her. Her car was out back where nobody parks. You know, at the very edge of the parking lot where there are so many trees."

"They haven't caught him yet?"

"No." Nicole blinked at a sudden thought. "Do you think this is why they called Wayne Hudnut out of second period?"

"Wayne and Millicent used to go out." Tracy gasped. "I'll bet Wayne did it. You read about that kind of thing in the paper all the time. Lots of times it's the husband that did it. Or else it's the boyfriend."

"That's ridiculous," Katie said. "If Wayne wanted to kill Millicent, why would he go to the mall to do it?"

"You don't understand, Katie," Tracy said. "These are *dark passions*!"

Suddenly the bell went off with a clang that made the girls jump, and they had to rush to their third-period classes.

As Katie reached the classroom, she felt her eyes fill with tears. The rows of desks in Mrs. Curtis's room, the map of the world pulled down over the blackboard, the struggling geranium on the windowsill—everything seemed so normal that it only made the horror of Millicent's death stand out more clearly. She hadn't meant for Millicent to die, Katie thought, her throat aching. It wasn't her fault. She groped frantically in her purse for a tissue. Dead! To think that while they had been at play rehearsal Millicent's body was already lying lifeless at the landfill!

The school buzzed all morning with the terrible news. When Katie met Steve in the cafeteria at lunch, she realized at once that he already knew.

He grabbed her arm roughly. "Somebody told me Millicent was strangled with a kind of thin rope or a cord. Is that true?"

"Stop it!" Katie cried. "Let go! You're hurting me!"

"Sorry," Steve said, abruptly letting her go. "There are so many wild rumors going around. I just can't figure out what's true and what isn't."

"What difference does it make?" Katie cried. "Millicent's dead. It's horrible! Just thinking about it makes me feel sick to my stomach."

"Of course it's terrible," Steve said perfunctorily. "I heard they found her at the landfill."

"That's what Nicole said."

"I wonder if they'll have any details on the news tonight."

Katie stared at her boyfriend. She had thought there was something going on between Millicent and Steve, but now she knew with a cold certainty that she had been wrong. Steve was not a bit upset by Millicent's death. In fact, he seemed more excited than anything else.

A new crowd of kids pushed into the cafeteria and reluctantly Steve got up to get in the lunch line.

"I wish you'd bring your lunch," Katie said. "By the time you get out of line lunch period's half over."

For a moment he stared at her as if he didn't understand what she was saying. "I would," he said at last, "but I can't live on bologna and Twinkies."

"I'm sure you could at least get hold of a Flakey's Fresh Chicken Salad," Katie said. "Your dad must have warehouses full of them."

"Don't even mention Flakey's," Steve groaned. "I get enough of that at home."

It had been big news in town when Steve's father had been brought in to replace the chairman of the board of Flakey's, a fast-food chain based in Rock Creek. Mr. Patton's position at Flakey's made him one of the most important people in town. Certainly, he was one of the best paid.

Katie sat down and began unpacking her fruit salad and cottage cheese. A moment later Nicole slid in next to her. "Are you planning to eat every bite of that," she asked, "or can I have some?"

"Help yourself." Katie pushed it over to her. "Take it all. I'm not hungry. I keep thinking about Millicent."

"I know," Nicole said. "Me, too. I'm not going out after dark until they catch whoever did it. What that nitwit Tracy doesn't seem to realize is that it could have been any of us. There's not much you can do to protect yourself when a maniac is running around loose. It really annoyed me to see her acting like she was too smart to get murdered." Nicole mimicked Tracy's tone. "'*I* always park under the light. *I* always lock my car. *I* could never be kidnapped.' As if anything you did could make any difference."

Katie lifted her eyes and looked at the blank, dusty windows of the cafeteria. She was dimly conscious of the high-pitched, meaningless chatter around her. Nicole was right. None of them were safe. "I used to think Steve was sort of getting interested in Millicent, but I guess I was wrong." Katie glanced at the lunch line. "He doesn't seem particularly upset."

"Of course not." Nicole snorted. "He's five feet eleven inches of sheer muscle. No chance anybody's going to strangle him."

"You think that's what it is?"

"What else?" Nicole stared at her friend. "What are you getting at, Katie?"

"I just thought he'd be more upset, that's all. I mean, he and Millicent did all those kissing scenes together in the play and all. Now she's . . . dead. You'd think he'd feel *something*."

"Boys are different," Nicole said crisply.

Nicole was right, Katie told herself. She was expecting Steve to react to the news the way she did, and that just wasn't going to happen. Guys were different.

"By the way," Nicole added, "somebody told me Wayne has an alibi. He had to fill in for his dad as a volunteer at the downtown shelter. Fifty alcoholic derelicts can swear he came in right after school. He made soup for everybody and didn't leave until two in the morning."

"The police actually thought Wayne did it?" Katie was startled. "That's the most ridiculous thing I've ever heard. Wayne is the sweetest, nicest boy. . . ."

"The police didn't think it was so ridiculous. And personally, I'm glad they're questioning everybody, because the sooner they catch this killer the better."

"Do you think they'll get him?"

"I don't know." Nicole shrugged uncomfortably. "What if it's some drifter who's living in a storm sewer someplace? How can they possibly expect to catch somebody like that?"

As if to illustrate Nicole's remark, a balding, middle-aged man in dirty overalls slouched toward them.

"Speaking of which—" Katie froze.

Nicole followed Katie's gaze. "That's no drifter, that's our new janitor."

"What happened to the old janitor?"

"He never did any work, so they fired him and got this new guy." Nicole's father served on the school board, and she always had the inside scoop. "Dad says he's a typical product of the sixties."

The janitor shuffled closer to them. "Hi there, Nicole." His smile showed a missing front tooth.

"Hi," Nicole said weakly.

After the janitor had passed by, Katie hissed, "How does he know your name?"

"Oh, I don't know. He knows Dad, I guess—and he's just really interested in the students. He used to go to school here."

Katie looked after him incredulously. "You're kidding me."

"Yup. Dad says he was pretty smart, too. Kinda weird, though."

"I can believe it. He looks like he crawled out from under a rock."

"He could use a bath," Nicole admitted. "Dad said when he went away to college he crashed and burned. Got into drugs and stuff. That's why he looks so awful. But he's clean now, and the school is giving him a second chance."

"I hope he doesn't try to get friendly with me." Katie watched the slack-jawed janitor push open the swinging doors to the kitchen. "He gives me the creeps."

"He's harmless enough. Your nerves are just on edge."

"You're right. I can't stop thinking about Millicent! You don't . . ." Katie's eyes sought Nicole's hopefully. "You don't have any psychic feeling about this, do you? I mean, it would be great if you could help the police."

"Well, I can't. I feel just like everybody else—sick." Nicole shuddered. "I've never known anybody who was murdered before. It's just so strange."

Katie leaned closer. "Are you sure you don't pick up any signals about this? Anything at all? An aura or whatever you call it?"

Steve put his tray on the table. "Hey, what's going on here?"

"I'm just encouraging Nicole to use any psychic gifts she's got to help catch this murderer."

"Sure. Go to it, Nicole." Steve's dark eyes were laughing at her. "Do your stuff."

"I guess you don't believe there's any such thing as a psychic, do you?" Nicole challenged him.

"I guess I don't. So sue me." Steve grinned.

"Well, go ahead and snicker, but not everything in the world can be explained in ten simple words, you know."

"I know. Look, I'm sorry I laughed, okay?"

"Apology accepted," Nicole said stiffly. She turned to her lunch, blocking out the sounds of Katie and Steve talking about the murder. As if that smile of his would solve everything, she thought resentfully. It was easy to see why Katie had fallen for Steve. He had it all—looks, brains, money, and that killer smile. But Nicole had never quite warmed to him. Steve might laugh at her psychic powers, but she did sometimes have these feelings about people, and she had a funny feeling about him. She sensed secrets behind his brown eyes, as if he was holding something back. There was a strange sadness under his smile, too, that was hard to describe.

Nicole bit her lip. Too bad psychic feelings couldn't be turned on and off like a television. A vague sense of dread had been with her ever since the murder, and the whisperings in her mind filled her with apprehension. The voices were muddled, as if they were coming from a cave full of echos. They gave her no hint of who had murdered Millicent. Pushing away the voices and the frightening mental image of Millicent's body, she got up suddenly.

"Are you leaving already?" Katie raised her eyebrows.

"Have to go to my locker," Nicole said shortly. As she was leaving, she heard Steve say, "She doesn't like me."

"Don't be silly," said Katie.

But Steve was right, Nicole thought as she made her way past some boisterous sophomores. She didn't like him. Only, she wasn't sure why.

Chapter Four

For scheduling reasons, Katie and most of the other drama kids were in Mr. Panovitch's English class after lunch. As they filed in, Katie noticed that the usually frenzied teacher was uncharacteristically sober. "I bet he's sorry," she whispered to Nicole. "He said that if Millicent was going to miss rehearsal she had better be dead."

"Is that what he said?" Nicole asked. "How awful!"

When class began, Mr. Panovitch did not mention Millicent's death directly, but Katie sensed it was very much on his mind. "Class, today we are beginning a classic of English literature—Shakespeare's *Macbeth*." Mr. Panovitch stared out the window. "Where was I?

Oh, yes, *Macbeth*. A story of ambition. And evil." He suddenly glared down at Katie as if she were personally responsible for the violence in *Macbeth*. "There is enough treachery and brutality in this story for even the most corrupt of you little people. Shakespeare was there long before *The Silence of the Lambs*. I want you to experience the play personally. Let it creep into your minds and hearts. Make a note of the assignment, dear people. I expect you to read it, and I mean read it—not watch the videotape."

Mr. Panovitch began to lecture about Shakespeare's life, and Katie's mind wandered. A mote of dust drifted downward in the motionless air of the classroom. The boy in the desk beside Katie twisted a paper clip until it spread out flat. Then he began scratching at the pencil groove on his desk with it. The class seemed interminable. None of us care about Elizabethan England, Katie thought. All any of us can think about today is Millicent.

She was relieved when at last the final bell rang and they got up to leave.

"Well, I know what I need." Nicole slammed her book shut. "A nice set of Cliffs Notes. I'm going to go to the mall tonight and get them."

Katie hesitated. "Did you say you were going to the mall?"

"Sure. Do you want to meet me . . ." Nicole stopped herself. "I forgot. The murderer. On the other hand, I may be reading *Macbeth* without the help of Cliffs Notes after all."

Katie glanced out the classroom windows. The autumn sun sent slanted rays through the clouds and the school building cast a shadow on the dry bristles of grass. "I wish it didn't get dark so early," she said.

That evening Katie sat in a pool of lamplight in the living room. As she struggled with the first few scenes of *Macbeth*, she thought longingly of the Cliffs Notes Nicole had mentioned. A summary of the scenes would come in awfully handy. The Elizabethan English seemed like a foreign language. By the time she figured out what the characters were saying, she had forgotten what was going on with the plot. And no matter how she tried to concentrate, her mind kept coming back to a murder closer at hand than the one in *Macbeth*. She squirmed restlessly for a moment, then got up and checked the back door to be sure it was locked. Pausing at the door a moment, she looked out into the darkness. The night outside seemed full of menace. Much as she might want to have the Cliffs Notes, she knew she could never go to the mall by herself.

"I guess no one has any errands to do at the mall," she said.

Mrs. Sloan poked her head out of the kitchen. "What did you say, Katie?"

"I need to go to the mall to get Cliffs Notes. I'm not getting that far with *Macbeth*. It's like reading Greek or something."

"You're certainly not going to the mall by yourself! You can forget that."

"I was hoping you or Dad could go with me."

"I expect your father will drive you. Can you do that, Philip?"

Mr. Sloan looked up from his newspaper. "I don't want to leave either of you here alone with a murderer running around loose. If we're making any trips to the mall, I say we all go together."

"I suppose you're right." Mrs. Sloan hastily dried her hands on her apron. "But I don't see how we can possibly go on living like this."

"It's just until they catch him. For a while we're going to have to be careful, that's all," said Mr. Sloan.

When they arrived at the mall, Katie noticed that the parking lot looked almost empty. Clearly, hers was not the only family that had been spooked by recent events. Once at the bookstore, she made a beeline for the corner where the Cliffs Notes were located.

"Don't bother to look for the Cliffs Notes." Nicole peeked out from behind a stack of self-help books. "Everybody else got here before us. Mrs. Marcus's classes started *Macbeth* last week. There's not a single copy left. They said they're getting a new shipment in a week or so, though. Did your whole family come with you?"

"You bet."

"Mine, too. Did you notice how empty the parking lot was? Only people as desperate as us are coming to the mall."

"I sure hope the police catch him soon."

"Don't count on it," Nicole said darkly. "Haven't you seen those TV shows they do about unsolved crimes? They never run out of new stories. That should tell you something."

It was almost ten when Katie and her parents got home. The light on the answering machine was blinking. Katie pressed the play button and heard a clear, high voice. "Katie? This is Laurie Wentworth. Would you give me a call? There's something I want to ask you about. It probably isn't very important, but—" Laurie's voice trailed off, then she hastily gave her phone number.

Katie glanced at the clock. Too late to call Laurie now. She and Laurie had the same algebra class, but they really didn't know each other very well. What could Laurie want to ask her? Probably something about the algebra homework, Katie thought, stifling a yawn. "I'm too tired to face Shakespeare," she told her mother. "I just hope Mr. P. doesn't give us a pop test tomorrow."

"Speaking of Mr. P.," said her mother, "I'm going to give him a call tomorrow morning. Until this madman is caught, I don't want you out at night by yourself. No more seven-thirty play practice for you. I'm sure all the other parents feel exactly the same way."

Katie didn't argue. She went again to the back door with its mullioned windows and tried the doorknob. It was still locked, just as it had been before they left the house. Uneasily, she gazed out the window. Past their yard, beyond the dark mass of the bushes and the drooping willow, she could make out the winking of the Allens' porch light, but between the house and that winking light was a great bowl of darkness. And somewhere in the silent darkness, a murderer was hiding.

Chapter Five

Dew was sparkling on the grass when Laurie Wentworth set out jogging the next morning. She was trying to trim her time in the mile by seven seconds. When she paused to tighten the laces of her running shoes, she could see her breath in the cool morning air. She always ran very early, before cars started pouring out of the subdivision on their way to work—she hated breathing exhaust fumes. She straightened up, did a couple of hamstring stretches, then jogged onto the golf-course path that ran closest to her house. Laurie ran the same route every morning. That way she could compare her times to see if she was getting faster. She was so familiar with the path that she didn't need to concentrate on where she was going. It was as if she were on automatic pilot and she was completely free to think.

This morning Laurie was focused on the phone call she had made the night before. Katie Sloan hadn't called her back. Not that it mattered. They would see each other in algebra this afternoon. Laurie just wanted to be sure she knew who the murdered girl was. She knew Katie would know, because they had both been in drama. Katie would be able to tell her if Millicent had owned a sheer green and blue skirt.

It was silly, really, but Laurie couldn't stop thinking about that bit of material fluttering in the breeze the other day when she had been jogging at school. It had looked like a scrap of sheer skirt stuck in the trunk of that car. Laurie had recognized it because she had seen one just like it at the mall. She would feel stupid calling the police about it, but they *had* said that anyone with any information should call them. She just wanted to double-check things with Katie, then she would call. Even though it wasn't likely that there would be any traffic at that hour of the morning, Laurie paused and looked both ways before crossing Green Tee Lane.

"Hey, Laurie!"

"What are you doing out here? I didn't know you lived in this neighborhood." Laurie didn't want to stop and socialize, but she hated to be rude.

"I don't, actually." The murderer smiled. "Here, I've got something for you."

"What?" Laurie drew back in surprise as he moved close to her.

He quickly slipped a cord around her neck. "This," he said, and pulled the cord tight.

Some minutes later there was a flash of light in the patch of young dogwoods at the edge of the golf course. Then the murderer returned to his car, which was hidden under some low-hanging trees. As he got in, he touched his shin gingerly. It looked as if he might have some bad bruises. Laurie had put up a terrific fight. Luckily, no one could fight long if their windpipe was being crushed.

Now she was no danger to him. But as he slowly drove away, he was annoyed. Killing her hadn't even been fun. She had only looked frightened for a second, and he had been too busy staying on his feet to enjoy it. She had been amazingly strong, not small and weak like Millicent. He grimaced. And she was as ugly dead as the others. He wished he could figure out a way to take the picture before they were dead. He wanted to catch that look of desperate fear in their eyes. Then he could pore over it again and again and feel the gut-deep thrill of pleasure that made his blood run hot.

He was careful about driving at precisely the speed limit and coming to a full stop at each traffic light. The last thing he wanted was to draw the attention of a cop. Not that there was any evidence against him. As far as anyone knew, he was just an innocent motorist. The body was miles behind him and hidden in the bushes. It might not be found for days. All things considered, taking care of Laurie had gone pretty well. But it nagged at him that he had yet to commit the perfect murder. Something always went wrong.

Scenery whizzed past his windshield. The perfect killing needed a lot of careful planning. Next time he wouldn't make the mistake of picking a member of the track team. He wanted someone less athletic, someone exquisitely pretty. He already had the girl in mind—he saw her every single day.

Katie. He smiled. He would love to see her terrified of him, conscious of his power. He licked his dry lips. Then, before she was dead and her face went slack and ugly, he would take the picture. He felt a flutter of pleasure low in his stomach. It would be a murder that would be fun to remember.

It would be the crowning touch to his work. He would show them all how they should be afraid of him. He hadn't decided yet whether he would strangle Katie or let her be blown to bits by the bomb he was making. But he was sure about one thing. This next killing would be his masterpiece.

He could see it now, the blood-splashed walls, the torn limbs, the shattered beams of the auditorium after his bomb went off. Newspapers all over the country would carry the story when he blew up the school on the play's opening night. Hundreds of the spoiled youth of Rock Creek High blasted into smithereens.

And Katie would be the first one to die. He chuckled softly.

Several hours later, Katie walked into Mr. Panovitch's English class. When she saw what was on his desk, she drew her breath in sharply and stepped backward, bumping into Nicole.

"What's the matter?" asked Nicole.

Wordlessly, Katie pointed to the desk, where a plump baby doll lay, covered only by the yellow Cliffs Notes on its belly. Skewering the Cliffs Notes to the doll was a large butcher knife that was red along its cutting edge.

"Gross!" Nicole moved up for a closer look.

Behind Katie, kids straggled into the classroom. She heard titters of nervous laughter.

"Guess he's sending us a message about Cliffs Notes," someone said.

Nicole, looking faintly green, sat down clumsily at her desk. "I think this is sick."

"The man is weird," said a voice behind Katie.

"Hey, let's at least give the dead baby a decent burial!" someone cried.

Katie hastily opened her paperback copy of *Macbeth*. She wished they were reading something lighter. Mr. Panovitch was right about *Macbeth*; it was full of evil. And the creepiest thing about it was that King Duncan's murderers were people in authority, people who were supposed to be trustworthy. People like Mr. Panovitch.

She looked up in alarm as the teacher strode into the room. The class suddenly fell silent. Katie found herself remembering Mr. Panovitch's comment about Millicent the other night. He had said that Millicent had better be dead if she missed rehearsal. And she was dead. For an awful moment Katie wondered if Mr. Panovitch had known that when he had spoken. He had been late to rehearsal, too. He could have killed her himself!

Mr. Panovitch stood behind the butchered doll, resting his fingers lightly on his desk. "You see," he said, "what I think of Cliffs Notes.

Now—" He took off his glasses and polished them absentmindedly with the corner of his handkerchief. "Since drama class is going to be preempted *again* by a pep rally this afternoon, I need to announce now that there will be no play rehearsal tonight. Future rehearsals will be held directly after school, beginning Friday. I am sorry if this creates problems for those of you who have other after-school activities."

"I've got cheerleading, Mr. P.!" cried a blond girl in the front row.

"I'm very sorry, Pamela, but if you cannot be excused from cheerleading on rehearsal days, then the chorus will have to limp along without you."

"Do I still get to come to the cast party?" she asked hopefully.

Mr. Panovitch ignored her. "My entire free period this morning was taken up with answering calls from concerned parents about the evening rehearsals, and I simply have no choice but to reschedule. We are all going to have to cope as best we can. Now, will you all please turn to act one, scene one?"

Katie's eyes were drawn back to the doll. Her stomach heaved. When the bell finally rang, Katie hurried out of the room. Mr. Panovitch could be a murderer, she thought, clutching her stomach. Millicent wouldn't have been afraid of

Mr. Panovitch. She trusted him. Judging by the mutilated baby doll, Katie was certain the teacher was not normal. He might be capable of anything.

The unnerving display in English class had left Katie more than a little bit upset. She got to algebra late and quickly scanned the room for Laurie, but Laurie's desk was empty. There was probably some perfectly reasonable explanation for Laurie's absence, Katie told herself. She either had the flu or had been called unexpectedly out of town—something like that. But Katie couldn't shake her feeling of uneasiness.

Class began and the teacher's voice droned on with the exact pitch and cadence of the school's air conditioner, a low monotonous hum. All Katie could focus on were inconsequential details like the chalk dust on Mr. Kildare's worn brown slacks or the birthmark on the back of Wayne Hudnut's neck. She wondered what Wayne was thinking. He and Millicent had gone together for a long time. He must have been reeling from the news of her death when the police brought him in for questioning as if he were a common criminal. It was awful. Katie didn't even like to imagine what he must have felt. She hadn't been at all close to Millicent, and yet she could hardly think of anything but the murder. Under the circumstances, going on with a normal school day as if nothing had happened was absurd.

As soon as Katie got home that afternoon, she called Laurie's number. The phone rang and rang, but no one answered. Katie glanced toward the open window at the darkness outside and shivered.

Chapter Six

As Katie was about to leave for school the next morning, the phone rang. She rushed back to the kitchen to answer it, wondering if it was Laurie. Instead, she heard her father's voice. Katie thought he sounded upset.

"What's the matter?" she asked. "Is something wrong, Dad?"

"Has Mom already left for work?"

"Yes, just a minute ago. She had to leave early. This is her week to drive car pool, remember?"

"Well, it's probably not important, but on my way to work I passed a bunch of police cars on Ridge Road right near Green Tee." He paused for a second. "I wish you weren't home alone. Why don't you call me when you get to school, just so I'll know you got there all right."

"It's broad daylight." Katie darted an anxious glance at the front door, which she had left ajar.

"I know," her father said. "Still, all those cop cars—I wish I had stopped and asked them what was going on."

"Maybe it was a car accident. I've got to run, or I'm going to miss the bus. Bye."

"Be careful!" Mr. Sloan's disembodied voice came from the receiver as she hung up the phone. Why would there be police cars on Ridge Road? It was a quiet neighborhood road that ran by the golf course—not a very likely place for a car accident, Katie thought.

She was careful to lock the front door behind her as she left the house. She saw something dark out of the corner of her eye and jumped. Almost immediately she realized it was only the tall holly tree beside the front entrance.

The grumbling roar of the school bus came closer and Katie ran for the street, her books clutched to her chest. The bus came to a halt with a groaning of brakes, and she scrambled aboard. The heat and noise inside the crowded bus enveloped her at once and she finally felt safe. As the bus lurched forward, she fell into a seat next to Nicole.

"Why do junior-high girls do such awful

things to their hair?" The very normality of Nicole's words jolted Katie. "Look at those two in the front." Nicole nudged her. "Talk about fashion victims—they look like they were plugged into an electrical outlet."

"Nicole," Katie said, "my dad saw a bunch of police cars on Ridge Road this morning!"

A paper airplane soared over their heads, but neither girl noticed. "It's probably nothing," said Nicole. "You've got to stop thinking about Millicent or you're going to go bonkers. I've decided I'm going to go on just like everything's normal. Maybe I won't go to the mall anymore, though."

"You mean just act like nothing happened when the guy who killed her is still out there somewhere?"

"How will it help if we freak out?" Nicole asked. "The police will catch the creep."

"You're right. I know you're right. I've got to pull myself together."

Both girls gazed out the window, as if reluctant to meet each other's eyes. They passed a strip of pine woods, the trees throwing eerie shadows in the pale morning light.

Nicole cleared her throat. "So do you think you're going to like taking over the leprechaun role?"

"I won't be as good as Millicent was." Tears

blurred Katie's eyes and she wiped them away with an impatient gesture.

"Don't think about Millicent." Nicole frowned at her. "Think of Steve and how nice it is to have those kissing scenes with him."

"I could kiss Steve whenever I wanted even before all this happened."

Nicole chewed on her thumbnail thoughtfully. "You know something, Katie? I think Bryan is getting ready to dump me. He didn't call again last night."

Katie was relieved that the conversation had turned to Nicole's boyfriend. The subject was safe and familiar. "He told you he was going to be busy this week."

"How can he be too busy to call? I'll bet he's after some other girl."

"It's probably your imagination. You ought to use your psychic powers. That way you could find out for sure if he has another girl."

"It's not that easy," Nicole said. "My psychic power is never there when I really want it."

In general, Katie didn't believe in things she couldn't see, but she tried to believe what Nicole said about her psychic powers.

"Why don't you just call Bryan?" Katie said.

"It wouldn't be the same. I want him to want to call me."

"Hey, give that back!" a junior-high girl screeched in Katie's ear.

"Make me!" a boy taunted as he jumped over to another seat.

"Stay in your seats!" the bus driver yelled, but there was no sign that anyone heard. Someone's homework spilled into the aisle. The noise level at the back seats rose. Buses full of sixth- and seventh-graders always came close to pandemonium, and Katie was relieved when the bus came to a halt at the junior high school and the younger kids poured out.

When the bus pulled away with a noisy screech, only a few passengers remained. Most of the time, the older kids drove their own cars or caught rides with friends. Riding the bus was generally regarded by high school kids as a kind of humiliation. But Katie was surprised at how comfortable it felt today to be on the creaky old bus with all its familiar sounds and smells. She gazed out the window and watched the trees go by. Then she turned to Nicole.

"Nickie, does Bryan talk about himself?"

"Constantly. He's always complaining about his mother. He says she says the same things over and over again, like 'Clean up your room' or 'Be nice to your little sister.'" Nicole shrugged. "It doesn't seem to hit him that he says the same things over and over again, too. I mean, if I've heard him complain about his mother once, I've heard it a thousand times. But that's still better than in the spring. Then all he talked about was baseball. I was getting to be an authority on the pitching problems of the Boston Red Sox." Nicole sighed. "I think I get your drift—you think I'd be better off without him. Maybe you're right. I should concentrate on looking at it that way—you know, sort of dwell on his faults. You think I should dump him before he officially dumps me, don't you?"

"No, it's not that," Katie said. "I was just thinking that Steve never talks about himself. I never hear about his parents or his sister, or even his dog. He just talks about what's going on at school. I've never even met his family."

"Maybe he thinks it would be bragging to make a big deal about his family. I mean, since his dad is boss of half the people in town and they have pots of money and everything. Steve may want you to love him for himself."

"I'll bet that's it." Katie remembered how Steve had said he was fed up with hearing about Flakey's. "It's probably tough being the son of somebody important."

"I wouldn't mind having his money, though."

"You can't say he flaunts it," Katie put in quickly. It was almost instinctual with her to defend Steve. She had grown accustomed to thinking of herself as half of a couple. She would have been happy to carry a sign that said, "I'm his and he's mine." She was that proud of him. But lately she had almost persuaded herself that there was something sinister about him. Her imagination was working overtime, she thought. That was the problem. She couldn't quite shake the feeling that he was hiding something. Why hadn't he ever told her anything about his old school and the town where he used to live? He acted as if his life had begun the day before he arrived at Rock Creek. It was very odd that he never said a word about his family. And Katie couldn't stop thinking about how excited he had seemed when he heard about Millicent's murder.

"If you really want to know what's on Steve's mind, why don't you ask Rage?" Nicole suggested. "Aren't they old friends or something?"

"Maybe I will."

The bus pulled into the parking lot at the high school and the girls got out, blinking a little in the sunshine. "Oh, no!" said Nicole. "There's Tracy. Let's go the other way."

Katie noticed that the girls with Tracy seemed upset—they were huddled together and one of them was crying. Katie clutched at Nicole's arm. "Something's wrong, Nickie." Then she saw the police car parked in front of the administration building. She knew with a cold certainty that someone else was dead.

"Tracy works in the office before school, doesn't she?" Nicole asked. "I'll bet she knows what's going on."

As the two girls approached, Tracy called out to them, "They found Laurie Wentworth's body on the golf course!"

Chapter Seven

"Laurie Wentworth. I can't believe it," Katie gasped. "She left a message on my machine the other night. I was going to ask her about it during algebra."

"What was she doing out on the golf course, anyway?" one of the girls asked.

"She just went out jogging!" Tracy's pale eyes were open so wide they seemed to bulge out of her face. "It happened early yesterday morning. I heard the police officer say the body was still warm when this guy found her. He was walking his dog, and the dog dashed off into the bushes and started barking and howling. That's how they found her so fast."

"You mean it happened in the daytime?" asked a small girl. "That's scary. But it was probably really deserted out there so early in the morning. She shouldn't have gone out on the golf course by herself. She should have stayed where there are lots of people."

"They're combing the whole golf course for clues," said Tracy. "That's what they told the ladies in the office. They're going over every inch of the grass."

Katie and Nicole exchanged a worried look. The golf course was in their neighborhood.

"I told Mrs. Smythe I just couldn't sit in the office making copies of stupid notices after what happened." Tracy sniffled loudly. "So she said I could go home if I wanted to, but I don't want to go home. I'd be all alone there with my parents at work, and you know what that means—he could be going after me next! Who knows how long he'd been watching Laurie, waiting for his chance?"

"Is that what the police said?" asked Katie. "Do they say he was watching Laurie?"

"They didn't actually say it," said Tracy. "But I can figure a few things out for myself. I've got a brain. He *had* to be waiting for her. You can't tell me he just happened to be out jogging and ran into her by accident."

"She's got a point," said Nicole.

"Laurie dead." Katie shook her head numbly. "I can't believe it."

The bell rang and Nicole and Katie reluctantly tore themselves away. They walked toward the classroom buildings in silence, their eyes fixed on the ground. Katie scuffed at the dry grass with the toe of her boot.

"Don't you think it's funny," she said, "two girls from the same school? Tracy's right, you know. The killer must have been waiting for her—that's why he knew where she went jogging. It could have been someone she knew." Katie suddenly stopped walking and stood still. "It could be somebody Laurie trusted," she whispered. She stared ahead at the raw, red brick of A wing. No one had ever called the utilitarian school buildings beautiful. Today they seemed cold and bleak.

"Maybe you'd better tell the police about Laurie calling you," said Nicole. "It could be important."

"But I don't really know anything. She probably just wanted to get the algebra assignment."

"I guess you're right," Nicole said doubtfully.

As the morning wore on, the news of Laurie's death spread quickly. Most of Katie's teachers were visibly upset. Mrs. Curtis was pale, and Katie could see her hands shaking. In Latin, Katie's teacher was so jumpy she could barely write the verb conjugations on the board.

The teachers weren't the only ones who were

shaken. Nicole pulled Katie aside in the hall between classes. "Katie," she whispered, putting her hand on Katie's arm and looking straight into her eyes. "You're in danger."

Katie's flesh rose in goose bumps. "What are you talking about?"

"I don't know." Nicole's hand tightened. "It's a feeling I got all of a sudden, an awful feeling. And I can sort of hear voices, but I can't quite make them out." She shivered. "I think it's Steve. He's dangerous. There's something funny about him."

Katie drew away. "You just don't like him, that's all," she said shortly. "And you're upset about Laurie."

"Listen to me, Katie!" Nicole pleaded. "It might be important."

"I've got to go. I'm going to be late," Katie said. "Pull yourself together."

"Katie, all I'm saying is be careful!" Nicole pleaded.

"We're surrounded by crowds of people. What can happen? I'm perfectly safe."

Nicole shivered.

"I've got to get to class," Katie said. "I really do." She gave her friend an uncertain smile and then hurried away.

As she was approaching her classroom, Katie reminded herself of the time that Nicole had predicted Mrs. Ennis's pop test. Should she be taking Nicole's warnings seriously?

The murderer watched the two girls talking in the hall. They were intent on what they were saying and oblivious to the traffic surging around them as their classmates rushed by. The murderer felt a strange flutter in his stomach. Maybe the girls were talking about him, he thought. Maybe he should kill Katie right now. His fingers twitched. The idea excited him so much he had to close his eyes and force himself to take deep, gulping breaths until his pulse stopped racing. He knew he had to stick to the plan. He would never get caught if he did that. Every detail was perfect. It wouldn't be long. Pretty soon he would allow himself to kill Katie. And later, maybe Nicole, too, although that wasn't exactly part of the plan. They wouldn't be able to whisper about him then, he thought.

All day, kids gathered in the halls in small groups to exchange meager snippets of information about the murders. Katie asked questions, but nobody was able to tell her more than she already knew. She could not shake the feeling of cold dread that Nicole's words had cast over her. What if Nicole was right about Steve? What if there was something wrong with him that didn't show on the outside? What if Steve turned out to be the murderer?

At lunchtime, Steve sat down next to Katie and a chill seized her. For a half second, looming over her, he had seemed threatening and Nicole's warnings had echoed in her ears. She edged her chair imperceptibly farther away from him.

"Well, don't everybody talk at once," Steve said finally.

"Laurie left a message on my answering machine the other night while we were at the mall," Katie told him. "Do you realize that I may have her last words on my answering machine?"

"Unless she spoke to the murderer," said Steve.

The idea that Laurie might have said something to her murderer gave Katie the creeps. But then, everything gave her the creeps today. Including Steve. She regarded her limp tuna fish sandwich with distaste. "Aren't you going to get in the lunch line?" she asked.

He frowned. "I'm not hungry."

"I'm not very hungry either. You can have my sandwich if you want." She pushed it toward him.

"Quit bugging me, Katie," he snapped. "Food's the last thing on my mind, believe me. I heard about Laurie on the radio this morning on my way to school. They said both of the girls were strangled with a cord. Do you think that's true?"

"What possible difference can it make?" Katie cried.

"A lot. I wonder if there's any other connection between the murders."

"Laurie and Millicent didn't even know each other. They were completely different—Millicent was the artsy type and Laurie was an athlete. They had nothing in common at all. Nothing."

"Except the way they died. Don't you see that Laurie's death is important? It sets up a pattern."

"You act like you're glad that Laurie got killed!"

"Don't be stupid. I'm not glad she's dead." Steve flushed. "Not exactly, anyway," he added under his breath.

Katie stared at him in horror.

"Heck, I didn't even know the girl, Katie. What do you want me to do? Break down and cry?"

"You could at least act like you're sorry," she whispered.

"Of course I'm sorry," he said shortly. "But I have to admit I'm interested in how it happened."

Katie jumped to her feet. "I can't sit here and

listen to this. Sometimes I feel like I don't even know you anymore."

"You don't have to get all holier-than-thou on me," snapped Steve. "It's no sin to be interested in a crime."

"Well, you can be interested in it without me." Katie blindly fled the cafeteria.

Once she was outside the building, she leaned against the door, breathing heavily. After a moment she became suddenly conscious of the eerie quiet around her. The campus seemed deserted. At this hour everyone was either in the lunchroom or behind the closed doors of the classroom buildings. Katie realized that although the campus held sixteen hundred people, in reality she was all alone.

Move, she told herself. But her feet seemed rooted to the spot. She couldn't make herself go back in the cafeteria to face Steve again.

Suddenly she heard a scraping sound on the pavement. Katie jerked around and found herself staring into the milky-blue eyes of the janitor. He gave her a snaggle-toothed smile. "Hiya, Katie," he said.

"How do you know my name?" she whispered.

"Oh, I like to get to know the students. Especially the pretty ones." He tried to laugh, but only managed a wheezing sound that broke off into a cough.

"Excuse me, I have to go." Taking a deep gulp of air, Katie bolted toward the classroom building.

As she rounded the corner, she ran right into Nicole. Katie threw her arms around her friend and burst into tears.

"Katie?" Nicole regarded her with alarm. "What's wrong?"

Katie pulled away, sniffling, and groped for a handkerchief. "I just had a fight with Steve and then I ran into the creepy janitor." She darted an anxious look over her shoulder, but there was no sign of him. "I'm so upset about Laurie and Millicent, I don't know what I'm doing. Two girls dead from this one school, Nicole! Doesn't it make you wonder—"

"We're all scared. But it didn't happen at school, Katie. It's probably just coincidence that Laurie and Millicent both went here."

"Maybe. I've been thinking of what you said about Steve." Katie hugged herself. "Do you really think there's something strange about him? You really think I should be afraid of him?"

Nicole nodded vigorously, and Katie's heart sank. "You never really liked Steve, did you?"

"How did you know?" Nicole asked. "I hoped it didn't show."

"Why? What is it you don't like about him?" Katie felt like she was pleading for Steve's life.

"I don't know. Like I said, there's something funny about him. For one thing, he's got a blue aura."

Suddenly the tension went out of Katie and she cracked up. She leaned against the brick wall and laughed until tears came to her eyes.

"I can't help it," Nicole said stiffly when Katie finally caught her breath. "I can see things that other people can't. Go ahead and laugh at me."

"I'm not really laughing at you." Katie wiped her eyes. "I'm just generally a mess. I've been so full of gloom and doom all day that what you said just hit me funny. I don't even know what I'm doing anymore. Everything seems so weird."

"Katie?" The quavery voice made Katie jump. She wheeled around to find herself face-to-face with the janitor, and again she froze. A couple of kids walked past. She reminded herself that she was perfectly safe. No one could hurt her with so many people around.

Grinning crookedly, the janitor held out a pencil. "You dropped this." Suddenly he was seized by a fit of coughing and Katie backed away from him. "Take it!" he said peevishly. "It's yours. You dropped it."

Reluctantly, Katie reached out for it. Her fingertips brushed against his hand, and she recoiled as if burned. The pencil, an old one, had her name embossed on it in gold letters. It was still warm from his touch. She knew she was going to throw it in the trash as soon as she got home. It was a favorite souvenir, left over from two dozen she had been given in the sixth grade, but now it felt polluted.

"It's got your name on it." The janitor giggled. "I bet I know where you live. You live over by the golf course, don't you?"

"I've got to get to English." Katie turned abruptly and ran. She didn't even care if people stared at her as she sped through the halls.

Nicole caught up with her just outside of Mr. Panovitch's class. Katie stood outside the door, not wanting to be alone with the teacher.

"I guess you're going to tell me the janitor is just a normal kind of guy, now," Katie said to Nicole. "I thought I was going to faint when he said 'I know where you live.' How can he know where I live unless he's been following me?"

"Maybe he knows your dad, just like he knows mine," Nicole suggested. "Maybe he looked you up in the phone book."

Katie took a deep gulp of air. "I wish he didn't know where I live. I really do."

Nicole peered into the classroom. "Just what I need right now. A big dose of

Macbeth," Nicole joked nervously. "I may die!"

"Don't say that!" Katie cried.

"It's just an expression," Nicole muttered.

During English class, it became evident that Mr. Panovitch was preoccupied. Although he didn't mention Laurie's murder, everyone knew that something was bothering him. He read from the book and didn't even try to embarrass anybody.

After English, Nicole took Katie aside. "I hear the school is getting a psychologist to come in and talk with students who've been traumatized."

"You think I ought to go, huh?" Katie looked at her friend seriously. "Maybe you're right. I'll go."

Chapter Eight

Katie was always early. It was an invariable habit with her—she couldn't shake the feeling that something would go wrong and make her late. So it was not surprising that she was usually the first to arrive at rehearsal. But this afternoon when she got to the auditorium she found Steve already there. He was sitting alone in the half-darkened theater staring at the stage. Katie hesitated when she saw him. She knew she was being irrational, but she didn't want to be alone with him. Face it, she told herself, you're afraid of him.

But Steve had already heard her and turned around. He flashed her a brilliant smile and waved broadly in a greeting. She went toward him hesitantly, but he eagerly held out his hand.

"I'm sorry," he said. "The fight at lunch was all my fault. I was concentrating so hard on figuring out the murders that I didn't realize how upset you were."

"I guess I have a short fuse these days," Katie said shyly, taking his hand. "It was just as much my fault as it was yours."

"So, are we friends again?"

"Sure." She smiled. "We're friends." She sat down next to him and felt much of her tension melt away.

"I can't stand it when you're mad at me," he said. She felt the light touch of his hand as he stroked her hair. "I hate it," he murmured. "I want to see a smile on that pretty face of yours."

The intensity in his voice troubled Katie and she found herself looking uneasily around the half-darkened auditorium. She wished someone would turn on the lights.

"I promised myself I was only going to go where there were lots of people—just to be safe. And now we're sitting here all by ourselves." She giggled. "Maybe it's not such a good idea."

Steve's arm enveloped her. "Hey, you know you're safe as long as I'm around," he said.

"Maybe." She laughed shortly. "But lately, I don't even feel safe surrounded by a crowd of my best friends."

"I'm not going to kiss you in front of a

crowd." He kissed her nose lightly, then turned her face toward him and pressed his mouth to hers. Behind her, Katie heard footsteps and book bags thudding to the floor and she knew the others were arriving. Someone had turned the lights on, and she could hear kids talking all around her. An uncomfortable twinge of fear fluttered in her stomach. What was wrong with her?

"Hey, break it up, you two." A metal hinge squeaked in protest when Nicole pulled down a seat in the row ahead of them and sat down. "I asked Mr. P. if he was going to call off rehearsal. But he said 'not a chance.' He said Katie needs all the practice she can get."

"Funny you should mention that," Steve said. "We just happened to be practicing the kissing scene."

"Sure you were." Nicole regarded him skeptically. "I told Mr. P. I thought it was pretty heartless to hold rehearsal today, and he had the nerve to say 'The show must go on.' The man is a complete cretin."

"You yourself said this morning that we all had to act as if nothing had happened," Katie pointed out.

"That was before we found out about Laurie getting killed," Nicole argued. "I wonder how many of us have to be murdered before it makes any impression on Mr. P. Knowing him, he'd probably just toss the bodies behind the curtain and use them as stage props. The man is too weird."

"You said it." Mike Green had leaned forward to join in the discussion. "He was one of the team teachers of European History. He did the literature. You should have seen how he loved the Great Plague. I never saw him that happy, except when he brought the picture of the dead Romanoffs to class. I bet he had to pry it out of a frame at home."

"Shh," said Katie, jerking her thumb toward the door. Mr. Panovitch bustled past them down the middle aisle.

"Let's get started, people," he warbled. "We have a lot of work to do. Okay, up on the stage, chorus. What are you toads waiting for? Mrs. Strawbridge can't make it today, so I'm going to serve at the piano. With my genius, of course, I can easily play and direct at the same time."

There was a crashing of the keys as Mr. Panovitch sat down at the piano. He began playing the lilting overture. Katie watched the choristers heading up to the stage. Rage looked so depressed it was almost comical. His head drooped and his footsteps dragged as he followed the gang up the stairs.

"Poor Rage. He hates being in the chorus,"

Katie said sympathetically. "I wish I could give him my part. It's not like I'm actually enjoying it."

"Be real. He wouldn't be any good as the queen of the leprechauns, and I hope you don't expect me to give up my part just to cheer him up," said Steve. "I'm not into self-sacrifice. Besides, he can't sing—"

"He doesn't have Steve's looks," Nicole chimed in.

"And Mr. P. certainly wouldn't like it," finished Steve.

And it was not as if Rage was a better actor than Steve, Katie thought. She had been surprised at first that Steve could act—it seemed too good to be true that anyone could be so cute *and* so talented. But when Steve got "into character" he seemed like a completely different person. Katie couldn't imagine how he did it. No matter what Mr. Panovitch said, no matter what hints Steve gave her about how to hold herself or alter the pitch of her voice, she never felt like anybody but Katie Sloan.

Nicole lowered her voice. "I hear they called off track practice. The track team's going to meet with a psychologist instead and talk about grief."

"I bet the janitor's disappointed," said Steve.

"Why?" Katie asked sharply. "Why would you say that?"

"Haven't you seen him? The guy is out there every afternoon watching the track team practice. Either he's the world's greatest fan or he's got some kind of track-shoe fetish. I think he comes to football practice some, too. Beats me how he gets his work done when he's so busy leering at people."

"He is working," said Nicole. "The faucets in the girls' bathroom are all polished."

"Just the same, I wonder where he was yesterday morning." Steve's eyes were narrowed.

"He's perfectly harmless," said Nicole. "My dad used to know him pretty well."

"Yeah, but that was a long time ago," said Steve. "People change. This guy has obviously gone downhill."

"He's just lonely," said Nicole. "That's probably why he hangs around the kids so much."

"You better get up on stage, Nicole," said Katie. "Practically everybody else is up there already."

"Oops! Right. I don't want Mr. P. to freak out." Nicole jumped up and trotted toward the stage.

"Is Nicole in love with that janitor or what?" Steve asked. "I just asked what he was doing yesterday morning and she comes down on me like a ton of bricks."

"Her father got him the job," said Katie.

"Oh," Steve said. "Well, I'd still like to know what he's been doing recently. And where he came from. Where did he live before he came to Rock Creek?"

Katie found herself thinking that she'd like to know those very things about Steve. His past was a blank. What could he be hiding? "You know," she said, "I'll bet Tracy could find out about the janitor for us. All that information must be in his personnel file in the office." She hesitated. "Now that you mention it, he is new around here and all of a sudden we've got two murders. I hadn't really thought about it that way before, but there could be a connection. If the murderer really did lie in wait for Laurie, then it must have been somebody who knew she went out running every morning."

"Anyone who knew she was on the track team would know that."

"Anyone from school would know that, you mean." Katie glanced up at Steve uneasily. She couldn't help thinking that he had moved to town about the same time as the janitor.

"Steve! Katie!" shrieked Mr. Panovitch. "Move it! We need to move along or we're going to be here all night, and your mommies and daddies wouldn't like that."

They leaped up at once and ran to their places. Once on stage Katie lined her toes up against the white chalk mark where she was to stand. She noticed that it had been smudged by Millicent's feet, and an image of Millicent being strangled sprang to Katie's mind. Overcome by the awful vision, Katie stood stiffly, her mouth dry. Suddenly she couldn't think straight.

Mr. Panovitch struck a crashing chord on the piano. "That was when you come in, Katie! Keep your mind on your job!"

Katie realized, too late, that she had missed her cue.

"Rage," shrieked Mr. Panovitch, "come down here and cue Katie. She's still new at this. Now, come on, people! Once more, this time with conviction! Be on your toes! All right. From Hegatha's entrance, people."

Rage got the script and sat cross-legged by the footlights. The open book on his knees reflected light on his pale, narrow face. Perversely, as soon as Katie knew he was there to cue her, she began to remember her lines. Even so, she knew her voice was wooden and mechanical. She found herself wishing she were as good an actor as Rage. He had been fantastic in *Twelfth Night* last year. Although he seemed reserved, Rage lost all his inhibitions when he was on stage. Katie could only dream of having that kind of talent. She couldn't even concentrate on the words she spoke, much less throw herself into it.

Mr. Panovitch jumped up from the piano shrieking. "Katie, is your mind in another country? Is that the best you can do?"

Katie jumped guiltily. "No, sir. I don't know, sir."

There was a murmuring in the chorus, and Katie heard Nicole say distinctly, "Only an idiot could concentrate on the dumb play when we're getting murdered one by one."

"Does the chorus have any thoughts they would like to share with me?" Mr. Panovitch said ominously.

Immediately the auditorium fell silent.

"All right, then. Let's start with the refrain of the leprechaun's dance."

Nicole's right, Katie thought as she moved into place for the dance. The serial killer isn't going to stop now. We're being picked off one by one.

Chapter Nine

The rehearsal seemed to last forever. When it was finally over, they all streamed off the stage sticky with sweat. Steve's arm around Katie felt heavy and hot. She wished he wasn't holding her so close; it made her feel claustrophobic. She wanted to push him away, but she knew it would only lead to an argument. She simply couldn't face another fight tonight.

"You'll get better when you're more comfortable in the role," Mr. Panovitch told Katie, looking none too confident. "I'm sure you will. Practice at home. Practice in your sleep. Practice, practice, practice."

"I keep thinking about Millicent," Katie explained.

"Don't!" he thundered. "The play is the

thing! Practice! Be brilliant!" He slapped the music down on the piano.

It was easy for him to say she wasn't supposed to think of Millicent, Katie thought darkly, but she was the one stepping into a dead girl's shoes.

"Come on," said Steve. "Let's go home."

The light from the exit sign tinged Steve's hand red as he reached out to push the door open. When they stepped outside into the chill twilight, Katie's teeth chattered and she thrust her hands into her jacket pockets.

"Cold?" Steve asked.

"Not really." She licked her lips and felt the cold air sting them. She was exhausted. That was why she was so nervous. "I'm pretty down about everything that's happened. I guess I could stand to go to the 'better land where the leprechauns live.'" She laughed shortly.

"Stupid play." Steve rested his hand lightly on the back of her neck as they walked toward the parking lot. She was conscious of voices calling to each other as the drama kids made their way to their cars. Suddenly, Steve's voice, close to her ear, made her jump.

"You know, I was upset that you misunderstood me at lunch." He looked down at her, his eyes dark in the twilight. "I'm not happy that two girls are dead, you know."

"I know, I know. I'm just so on edge. Everything is getting to me."

"All I meant is that if there's a pattern to the killings, it should make it easier to find the murderer. And it's crucial that this guy be brought to justice."

"Oh, I know!" Katie spoke too fast in her eagerness to agree with him. "I—I feel exactly the same way. I thought you seemed kind of cold-blooded about the murders, but people have different ways of dealing with things. I can see now that we really feel the same way. We just express it differently." She could hear the wheedling note in her voice, and she hated herself for it. But she felt she simply couldn't bear it if Steve got mad at her again.

He frowned. "It's a really personal thing with me—justice. I don't mean the system of law and order we have around here, I mean real justice."

"But isn't justice the same thing as law and order?"

"No," he said shortly. "Justice is a higher law."

"But nobody's above the law, are they?" She met his eyes anxiously, wondering what he was getting at.

"It's too complicated to explain." He took her hand. "Let's go by Burger Heaven and get ourselves a big cookie."

"Not to Flakey's?"

"Definitely not Flakey's."

Katie still couldn't believe that Mr. Patton would be happy to have his son openly patronizing a competing fast-food chain. Steve's relationship with his father seemed off-key to her. Something in the tone of his voice made her wonder, sometimes, if they didn't get along. "I can't stay too long," she said. "If I'm not home on time, my dad will worry. He actually made me call him from school to let him know I got there all right. I called after homeroom, but I don't think it was very reassuring—I had to tell him about Laurie."

Katie sank into the low seats of Steve's sports car. The car hugged the road tightly as they sped out of the parking lot. Katie wondered why he was driving so fast. He was usually very careful about staying within the speed limit, as if he were afraid of being stopped by a cop. Or was she imagining things again? When she glanced over at Steve she saw that he was frowning. She didn't know what to say, so they drove in silence.

When they got to Burger Heaven, Katie began to feel more relaxed. She tried to avoid talking about the murders, but she soon discovered Steve wasn't interested in any other subject.

"If we could just get close to the police investigation," Steve said, "then we'd have a better idea of what was really going on. The newspaper accounts are so sketchy. In a small town like this, we ought to be able to find somebody who knows what the police have been up to. You've lived here your whole life, Katie. You must know somebody who has a cop in the family."

She shook her head. "Nope. Nobody."

"Or even a secretary at the police station? When you think about it, every bit of evidence, everything that anybody says to the police, has to be typed up and filed by somebody."

"Darren Scott's mother used to work for the traffic division, I think," Katie offered. "I don't know if she still does, though."

"It's a start. Where can I find this Darren Scott?"

Katie hesitated. "Why do you want to?"

"So I can find out what the police know. I told you that."

"As long as they catch the murderer, what difference does it make how they do it?"

"Justice is everybody's business. Look, we aren't going to have another fight, are we?"

Katie quickly shook her head. To her relief, the door swung open and Nicole and Bryan walked in. Katie jumped up and waved at them. She wanted someone else at the table to ease the tension between her and Steve. The excitement in his eyes when he spoke of the murders troubled her more than she liked to admit. She didn't understand why he was so interested in the killings. It wasn't as if he was frightened the way she was. Why couldn't he talk about something else?

A moment later Nicole and Bryan put their tray on the table and slid into the booth. "Hola, Steverino," said Bryan. "What's up?"

"You've been talking about the murders, haven't you?" Nicole darted a quick look at Katie. "Let's not talk about that."

"Oh, don't be stupid, Nicole." Steve frowned. "What's the point in not talking about it if everybody's thinking about it anyway?"

"What I hear," said Bryan, "is that if you get pressure on the carotid artery, like when you get a cord tightened around your neck, you pass out right away, so chances are Laurie didn't feel a thing."

"You're making me sick." Katie pushed her food away.

"Has anybody heard anything new about what happened?" asked Steve.

Bryan shook his head. "Just rumors. A lot of weird things are going around school. I've even heard that Millicent and Laurie were involved in a satanic cult."

Nicole snorted.

"I said it was rumors," Bryan told her. You know how it goes. People will say anything. The weirder it is, the faster it goes around."

"I think it's terrible to say bad things about people after they're dead and can't defend themselves," said Katie.

Bryan grinned. "Oh, they'll say bad things about living people, too."

"Bri's right," Nicole said. "That's just the way gossip is."

"It's sick." Katie was unable to control the tremor in her voice. "People like to think there was something unusual about Millicent and Laurie. They think that there should be some reason they got killed. But there wasn't anything unusual about them! They were just like us!"

"I didn't say I believed all that junk people are saying," said Bryan. "I agree with you all the way."

Katie's eyes blurred with tears. "I think I'd better go home." She leaped up, dumped her tray in the trash, and headed toward the exit. Steve didn't follow her, and she hesitated at the door, looking out at the twilight-darkened parking lot. She could hear Steve asking Bryan and Nicole if they knew Darren Scott. Didn't he realize that if people knew he was snooping into the police investigation they were going to wonder? The next thing she knew, rumors could be going around about Steve.

A minute later Steve joined her at the door. He put his arm around her shoulders and smiled down at her. Katie stared into his eyes, feeling a flutter of attraction. The cool perfection of his looks made her feel weak at the knees even now. How could she even think that he might be a murderer?

"I'm glad you didn't go dashing out into the parking lot without me," Steve said softly. "These days you can't be too careful."

Her eyes met his. "Steve—" she began.

"What?" His voice hardened.

She quickly looked away from him. "Nothing." For a moment she'd thought he would say something to make her feel close to him again. But then she realized it wasn't going to happen. The murders stood between them like a wall.

Sighing, Katie pulled the door open and stepped out into the cold darkness. She knew she was overreacting because of the murders, but she couldn't help feeling that Steve seemed almost sinister lately.

A harsh wind blew across the parking lot, making bits of trash turn cartwheels along the pavement. The small hairs on the back of Katie's neck stood on end. She was afraid, she realized bleakly.

She was afraid of Steve.

Chapter Ten

The next morning it was announced that therapists were going to meet with worried students in small groups. Katie signed up to go fifth period. At this point, she would do just about anything to get out of Mr. Panovitch's class. Lately the drama coach upset her so much she could hardly stand to be around him.

Katie headed to the media center after lunch. On the door was a sign reading, "Grief and Stress Management—Appointments not necessary." She stepped inside and found that chairs had been arranged in a circle near the college catalogues. Several girls had already arrived and were talking in low voices.

Katie was surprised to see Rage follow her into the room, looking even paler than usual in the fluorescent lights of the library. He found a place two seats over from her, crossed his arms, and glowered at the group. She wiggled a few fingers in a halfhearted greeting and he answered with a grudging nod of his head.

Katie wondered if Rage felt uncomfortable about being the only boy in the group. She thought it was cool of him to show up. Lots of guys wouldn't like to admit they were upset enough to talk to the therapist. He looked relieved when some other guys came in, a blond boy whom she recognized as the band drum major and a dark-skinned boy who was growing a moustache. She vaguely remembered the dark boy with the fuzzy upper lip from drama class last year.

People kept coming in until all the chairs were filled. Most of the guys perched on the library tables, keeping a slight distance from the girls.

"I almost didn't come to school today," said a girl with thin lips. "But my dad said it's better to keep to the routine. He said he learned that in the army. Even if you're about to go into battle the next day, you have to shine your shoes and clean up your tent. It's the routine that keeps you from falling to pieces."

"Nothing can keep me from falling apart," said the girl next to her. "I've never been so upset in my life. It is like living in a war zone. We don't know who's going to be the next to die."

Wayne Hudnut came in, his sad eyes seeming out of place in his wholesome-looking, ruddy face. He stood in the doorway for a moment and then said awkwardly, "It's pretty crowded. I'll go look for some chairs."

"That was Millicent's ex-boyfriend," one of the girls whispered. "The police had him in for questioning."

"He was completely cleared," Katie said. "He had a perfect alibi."

"They always do," said the girl.

It was a strange gathering, Katie thought. Everyone was frightened and everyone looked pale. The boys sat aloof on the long table, their arms folded, trying to fake an air of calm unconcern. The girl with pinched lips plucked nervously at her jeans, while her friend dabbed at her eyes with a tissue.

At last the therapist arrived. She was a tall, middle-aged woman with horn-rimmed glasses perched low on her nose. She wore a turquoise pendant and a dress that looked as if it had been woven on some peasant's loom.

"I'm Dr. Philpot," she announced.

"And I'm here to help you," Rage muttered savagely.

Katie wasn't sure Dr. Philpot heard his remark. At any rate, her poise was unruffled. "You're all under a lot of strain," she said, "and I think it may help if you talk about your feelings."

Wayne staggered in the door carrying a stack of chairs.

"I wonder what he's trying to prove," one of the girls said.

"Let's put them over here." Dr. Philpot gestured largely. "Just make yourself comfortable wherever you can find a place to sit."

"I want you to remember," Dr. Philpot continued, "that there's no right or wrong way to feel. Sometimes it makes us feel better to share our emotions, whatever they are."

Katie stared at the woman in amazement. This was supposed to help? If this was the way the session was going to be, Katie thought it would be a waste of time. What good was talking? Even if Dr. Philpot could have waved a wand and made their fears disappear, it wouldn't help the situation. Fear was their best protection against the murderer. Fear made them careful. The only other thing that would help was finding the murderer.

"Now, where would you like to begin?" Dr. Philpot clasped her hands over her knee and regarded them blandly.

"I want to know who does this kind of thing." Rage's voice seemed unexpectedly loud in the tense silence. "Could somebody look and act normal and be doing this?"

"What a creepy thought!" one of the other girls said nervously. "I mean, you know he's got to be insane!"

"Do you?" Rage countered.

"Well, isn't he?" The girl shot a challenging look at Dr. Philpot.

"Of course, I can't really say anything about the murderer until he or she is caught," said Dr. Philpot. "We just don't know."

"*She?*" cried the thin-lipped girl, horrified. "You're saying it could be a girl?"

"We just don't know," repeated Dr. Philpot. "Maybe that's what's bothering us, in part. This danger is unnamed, unknown. That makes it more frightening. We don't know what to look out for, so we don't know how to protect ourselves. Maybe we have to even face the fact that there is no sure way to protect ourselves. That's a scary thought."

"I never go out after dark now," said a girl with glasses. "And I try to stay with groups of people. I don't go places alone anymore."

"We naturally take extra precautions, but even then we may not feel quite safe."

There was a long silence as Dr. Philpot's

words seemed to echo in the room. Safe? Katie thought. She could scarcely remember when she had felt safe. That feeling belonged to a long-ago part of her life, along with the tooth fairy.

"Does anyone miss Millicent and Laurie?" Dr. Philpot went on. "Is there, in some sense, a hole in our lives now that they are dead?"

"I dream about Millicent." Wayne flushed painfully red when everyone looked at him. "In the dream she's not doing anything. She's just standing there and, you know, it's just nice to have her there and I wake up and then I feel awful when I realize it's just a dream."

"A common grief reaction," Dr. Philpot assured him. Her voice was creamy and soothing. "It's hard to say good-bye to those we have loved."

Wayne looked even more heartbroken. This session isn't helping anybody, Katie thought miserably.

"It's not fair! She was just sixteen!" another girl cried, promptly bursting into tears.

Dr. Philpot held out a box of tissues. Katie noticed she had the large, economy size.

"I just get so mad," sniffled the girl. "Nobody's doing anything. The murderer is getting away with it!"

"I wish it were a dream," Katie said. "And I could wake up and everything would be back the way it was. I had algebra with Laurie, and I just can't believe somebody killed her. She was a real nice girl."

"It's scary when bad things happen to good people," said Dr. Philpot. "Sometimes it seems as if everything is falling apart. We have to remind ourselves that a lot is still right with the world. Even in the most awful situation there are some things that are wonderful—our friends, for example. Clean sheets. Mozart."

Katie stared at her silently. Clean sheets were supposed to be a comfort when they were being stalked by a murderer?

"Great," Rage said ironically. "I've got to remember that stuff about clean sheets."

By this time several of the girls had burst into tears. Dr. Philpot stood up and placed a piece of poster board on an easel. "Danger signs of depression," Dr. Philpot read. She began going down the list one by one—difficulty sleeping, change in appetite. Her voice droned on, but Katie barely heard her. She had tuned Dr. Philpot out. What difference did it make how they felt about it? It was no good for them to sit around bursting into tears and reassuring each other while a strangler killed them one by one.

The bell rang, and to Katie's surprise many of the students stayed on to speak to Dr. Philpot individually. Katie headed for the door. "Wasn't that session the worst?" she asked Rage when they were outside. A chill breeze brushed her cheek, and she shivered.

"She didn't really answer any of our questions," Rage said. "She just kept repeating what everybody said."

"Being a psychologist must be easy, all right. I could have done that." Katie fumbled with her books and darted a quick look up at his face. "Why did you ask her about the kind of person who did it?"

Rage shrugged. "I wondered. Don't you?"

"I just thought maybe you had a particular reason."

"Just curious."

A gust of wind blew dry leaves against the brick with a whispering rattle. Wayne Hudnut came out the door and smiled at them. Katie did her best to smile back, but it took a conscious effort to relax and make her breathing regular. She wheeled around and faced Rage.

"You and Steve were friends from way back, weren't you?" she asked.

Rage looked uncomfortable. "Look, I better get to class. See you."

He hurried off. Disappointed, Katie watched him leave. Rage was obviously in no hurry to talk about Steve. If there really was some mystery about Steve's past, it was obviously going to be difficult to drag it out of his loyal friend.

Chapter Eleven

The days after Laurie's death seemed to pass very slowly. Every morning, Katie grabbed the newspaper expecting to see that the police had made an arrest, but every day it was the same—nothing.

The following week it was Katie's turn to have the family car. Her mother drove the car pool one week a month, but on the other weeks Katie had the car to drive to school. In the past she'd always been relieved to have the car. She had celebrated the day she got her license, knowing she could look forward to being free of the school bus. But riding alone to school was suddenly not very appealing. On Sunday night Katie called Nicole and offered to give her a ride.

"Thanks," said Nicole, "but I'm catching a ride with Bryan. Now that he's finished with his history paper, he says he wants to make up for lost time and spend every minute with me. Isn't that sweet?"

"I'm really happy for you," Katie said in a hollow voice. It was stupid to worry about driving to school alone, she thought. It would be broad daylight and she could lock her doors.

"You're being careful, aren't you, Katie?" Nicole asked anxiously.

"Why? Why do you ask?" Katie said, although she already knew what Nicole was getting at.

"I had such an awful dream last night," said Nicole. "I woke up at two in the morning, and I was so scared I almost called you."

"It's a good thing you didn't. My parents wouldn't have liked it."

"Well, I didn't, did I? I just sat there in a cold sweat thinking that you were dead."

Katie shivered. "Hey, thanks a lot for sharing that with me, Nicole. You really know how to cheer a person up."

"I can't help it. It was awful. And on top of it I keep hearing these voices in my head, and I can't make out what they're saying. It's like people in a cave or something all talking at once."

"If you can't hear what they're saying, then

how can you be sure they're saying I'm in danger?" Katie asked reasonably. "Maybe they're just trying to warn you a pop test is coming up."

"No!" said Nicole. "I know you're in danger. I may not be able to hear exactly what they're saying, but I'm sure you're not safe. That's why I almost called you. But then I thought, what can happen to you when you're home in bed? So then I felt better."

The curtains of Katie's bedroom window blew suddenly in a gust of wind and she jumped. The receiver clattered to the floor. Katie lunged at once for the window, slammed it shut, and locked it.

"Katie? Katie?" Nicole's voice sputtered from the receiver on the floor.

Katie grabbed the phone. "I'm here. Sorry. I had to close the window."

"Don't do that to me!" cried Nicole. "I thought the strangler got you. You scared me to death!"

"Sorry," Katie said shortly.

"Well, just be very careful."

"I am careful! I'm as careful as I can possibly be!"

"All right."

"All right, then. Have a nice time with Bryan," Katie said. Then she slammed the receiver down. Nicole had made her so upset she could hardly think straight. What was she supposed to do? It wasn't like she could have six bodyguards from the football team. And even if she could, there was no guarantee one of them wouldn't turn out to be the strangler. She wished Nicole hadn't told her about the voices. Sometimes she felt as though she was hearing things herself. The brush of a drapery against the floor, the faint hum of the clock in the kitchen, the rustle of newspaper—these faint sounds were suddenly full of hidden meaning, as if the house itself were trying to tell her she was in danger.

Katie heard footsteps in the driveway and looked out the window. Her mother was back from the grocery store. Normally Katie would have jumped to open the door for her, but something held her back. She went into the kitchen and watched in silence as her mother's key turned in the lock. "Mom?" she called in an uncertain voice.

The door flew open and her mother staggered in with two bags of groceries. "The other two bags are in the trunk, Katie. I left it unlocked."

"I'll get them," Katie said, wishing her father were home. She felt vulnerable the moment she stepped into the shadowy garage. The single light bulb high on the rafters wasn't enough to dispel the gloom. Katie quickly went to the wide-open trunk and picked up the bags. An egg carton was poking out of one, and the other was heavy with a gallon of milk and a bag of oranges. Katie balanced the heavy one on her hip while she slammed the trunk closed. As she turned toward the door, a shift in the light drew her eyes up to the rafters. To her horror, Katie found herself staring at a mutilated baby doll dangling from a noose. The plastic doll swung gently back and forth, its rosebud lips and round baby head a bizarre contrast to the thin rope that encircled its neck.

The grocery bags slipped from Katie's nerveless arms. She was vaguely conscious of the crash of eggs and of oranges rolling on the cement floor as she screamed.

An hour later, Katie's father hung up the phone and surveyed his worried family with a frown. "Panovitch says he tossed the doll in the Dumpster at school after he was finished with it."

"Do you think he was telling the truth?" Katie asked anxiously.

"I certainly can't imagine George Panovitch pulling out our extended ladder and getting that doll up on the rafters," Mr. Sloan said.

Katie could see her father's point. It was hard

to picture plump, prissy Mr. Panovitch up on a ladder.

"I'm going to call the police," said Mr. Sloan. "I think they ought to know. After two murders, that doll is like a threat. There's the off chance it might be connected. But realistically, I have to say it's probably just some kid's idea of a joke. Somebody fished that doll out of the Dumpster and decided it would be cute to scare us to death."

Mrs. Sloan shuddered. "The idea that some stranger was poking around in our garage really gives me the creeps."

"If it was a joke, it was in remarkably bad taste," Mr. Sloan said grimly. "Just the same, I'm going to take the doll into the police station tomorrow."

"Dad?" Katie asked in a small voice. "Would you move Mom's car out front for me? I don't want to go in the garage tomorrow morning when I leave for school."

"Sure thing." Her father gave her a hug. "It was just a stupid joke, Katie. Don't let it get to you."

"Taking the doll to the police is just a precaution," Mrs. Sloan said soothingly.

"Right. Just a precaution."

They all smiled unconvincingly at each other.

Chapter Twelve

The light was thin and gray when Katie went out to the car the next morning. All color seemed to have bled out of the sky. The grass and sidewalks were dank with dew, and beads of condensation covered the car. Katie looked around nervously, wishing there were more people out on the street. The neighborhood seemed forlorn and empty. She reminded herself that behind the closed blinds of nearby houses were people getting ready for work, children gathering books for school. Her mother's car pool would be along any minute.

Millicent and Laurie had probably felt safe and normal, too, Katie thought. They had probably started their last days just like she was starting today. Hesitating a moment with the keys in her hand, Katie suddenly turned back and opened the trunk. Groping under the stiff material that lined the bottom, she fished out the tire iron. When she got into the car, she laid it beside her on the front seat. She felt a little silly, but it was good to know that she had a weapon close at hand.

At school, she found Nicole and Bryan sitting on the edge of the brick planter in front of the administration building. They were staring at each other and seemed completely oblivious to everyone else around them. Katie waved her hand in front of Nicole's face to get her attention.

"Oh, hi, Katie." Nicole smiled dreamily. "There's no rehearsal this afternoon because Mr. Panovitch has to go to a special faculty meeting. Bryan and I are going to the movies." She beamed.

Katie immediately thought of the doll in the garage. She didn't want to be home alone again today. Nicole was no help, so Katie went looking for Steve. She found him by the auditorium. "I guess you heard there's no play practice," she said.

"Yeah, it's posted. I wonder what this emergency faculty meeting is about."

"You think they know something about the murders?"

"I wish I knew."

"Maybe they're arranging for more therapists to come to school and help us talk about our feelings," Katie said bitterly. "How'd you like to do something after school? Since we don't have practice, I mean. I'm not that crazy about going home to the empty house, to tell you the truth."

"I can't." His eyes were apologetic, but he didn't explain.

"Oh, well, if you can't." Katie shrugged. Maybe she shouldn't be alone with Steve anyway, she thought, remembering how frightened of him she had been the other night. Of course, if Steve had wanted to kill her, he had already had plenty of chances.

"Just keep your doors locked and you'll be okay."

She gave a little laugh. "Yeah, it's just getting from the car to the house that worries me." Katie thought of telling Steve about the doll, but something held her back. He had been acting so strange lately that she wasn't sure she wanted to see his reaction to this latest occurrence.

"Go home with Nicole," Steve suggested.

"Nicole and Bryan are going to the movies—are you sure you can't . . ."

"I just can't, Katie. I'm sorry."

She started to ask him why, but the words

died on her lips. It was obvious that he didn't want to tell her. Another of the little mysteries that always surrounded Steve. How could she ever have thought they were close?

On the way to homeroom, Katie noticed the janitor standing by the lockers with a broom. Katie felt a chill run down her spine. Why was he trying to sweep when the halls were crowded with kids? She knew he just wanted an excuse to watch them all. No matter what Nicole said, Katie didn't trust the janitor. She felt safe only when she was in her classroom. At least he couldn't follow her inside.

While Mrs. Curtis droned on with the announcements, Katie wondered what Steve was doing after school. There were so many things he didn't want to tell her. Maybe that was what made her think he had a secret life. At school he was the dashing new boy with the black sports car. At home he was—what? She couldn't imagine.

"Mrs. Curtis?"

The hoarse voice made Katie jump. The janitor was standing at the classroom door with his broom.

"Could I speak with you a moment?" he asked.

"Uh, of course," Mrs. Curtis stammered, pushing her chair back from her desk with a clatter.

Katie wanted to scream "Don't go out there

with him!" but she was more afraid of making a fool of herself than she was of the janitor. After all, it wasn't too likely that the janitor would call Mrs. Curtis out in the hall and then promptly kill her.

But still Katie was relieved when Mrs. Curtis, blushing hotly, came back in the classroom five minutes later. The bell rang and Katie's classmates jumped to their feet. "The announcements are posted in the office," Mrs. Curtis shouted over the commotion. "Club members please check the office bulletin board."

As the others surged out of the classroom, Katie hung back. She stood silently at Mrs. Curtis's desk until the teacher looked up at her. "What is it, Katie?"

"Do you know him, Mrs. C.?" Katie asked. "The janitor, I mean."

"I used to. We were in high school together."

"It's really hard to believe he went to school here."

Mrs. Curtis buried her face in her hands. "Oh, Katie, I hope you never have to see an old friend fall on hard times. Poor Hugo. He was such a nice boy. A little unusual maybe, but really nice underneath. Now his health is gone, his education wasted. . . . It's just horrible."

"What did he want to talk to you about?"

Mrs. Curtis straightened up and took a deep

breath. "It's these murders. Poor Hugo is afraid he's going to be suspected. He kept asking me over and over if I knew anything." Mrs. Curtis clumsily groped for a tissue in her large purse and blew her nose. "Of course, people are bound to talk just because he looks so odd. Years as a street person, living out of Dumpsters, suffering from hepatitis, all those things have left their mark. I've heard the students say they were afraid of him." She cast a nervous glance at the door. "Of course, I didn't tell him that."

"What did you say his name was?"

"Hugo. Hugo Clements."

"When they catch the murderer, it'll be a lot easier on everybody," said Katie.

"You are so right." Mrs. Curtis sighed heavily.

Katie hurried out of the classroom. She was going to be late for her first-period class, but it had been worth it. So the janitor knew that the kids were suspicious of him! Why did he hang around staring at them, then? He must know it would frighten them. Maybe his brain was so muddled he didn't make the connection.

During study hall, Katie got permission to go to the library. She went straight to the shelves where the old yearbooks were kept. She leafed through the yearbooks looking for Hugo Clements's picture. Mrs. Curtis had been out of high school at least twenty years, she figured. At last she found him in the 1969 edition. *Hugo Clements—Pep Club, Tri-Hi-Y, Math Club, Science Club.* A thin-faced brunette boy looked soberly at the camera. *Fondest memory—All the great times we had in the photo lab—har, har. Ambition—To be a rambling wreck from Georgia Tech and a heck of an engineer.*

Katie closed the yearbook feeling shaken. How had the kid who was Hugo Clements turned into the sinister janitor? It was like some horribly twisted fairy story where the earnest young prince turned into the wicked toad.

After school, Katie didn't go home. She was afraid of her empty house. She thought about going to the mall instead, until she remembered that Millicent had been abducted from there. She decided to go to Flakey's. It would be full of people and as safe as anywhere else in town.

As she pulled into the parking lot she was immediately reassured by the sight of children playing in the restaurant's playground. She could hear the children's piercing squeals of delight as they went down the slide. She went inside, ordered fries and a drink, and took her tray to a table that overlooked the playground. It was good to be in a brightly lit, public place. "Welcome to Flakey's. May I take your order?" The words were a comforting litany. It was safe. She pulled out her algebra book and began working the even-numbered problems.

A few minutes later she spotted Rage coming in and waved at him. "Come sit with me!" she called.

Rage looked uncomfortable, but he nodded as he went up to the counter. Katie smiled to herself. She knew he was afraid she was going to pump him about Steve. Well, too bad. She was determined to worm the truth out of Rage one way or another.

A few minutes later, he put his tray down on her table and sat down. "I almost didn't recognize you without Steve," he said. "I thought you guys were joined at the hip."

Katie blushed. She supposed she had been clinging to Steve a lot lately. "You know you'll never run into Steve at Flakey's, Rage. He doesn't come here."

"No?" He raised his eyebrows. "Why not?"

"You tell me. You've known him longer than I have," Katie said.

"Maybe he knows something about what they put in the hamburgers."

Katie folded her hands and regarded him with quiet determination. "Rage, what was it like to know Steve in his old town?"

"It was an honor."

Katie wasn't sure she had heard him right. "What do you mean?"

"Well, you know Steve—looks, brains, money. Girls fall all over him, grown-ups love him. I just sort of trailed along in his shadow. Of course, I was only there during the summers, so I didn't go to school with him or anything."

"But you used to hang out together, didn't you?" Katie had already decided not to ask about Steve's family right away. Better to lead up to it gradually.

"Oh, sure, I guess," said Rage. "We caught tadpoles, played around construction sites, built a clubhouse. That kind of thing. Then, when we got older, Steve got real busy—you know, fending off all these girls. But we still played tennis now and then. Steve's a really good tennis player. No surprise. He was born with a silver racket in his fist."

"It sounds like you were jealous of him."

"Me, jealous because Steve had everything? Heck, no. I rise above all that stuff." His gaze wandered to the children playing outside.

"I get jealous of Nicole sometimes too," Katie confessed. "Lately she's so cool and I'm a bundle of nerves. And she's so pretty. . . ."

"You're pretty, too, Katie."

Katie blushed. "And—and Nicole has these psychic powers and everything, too," she stuttered.

"You're putting me on."

"No. Really, she does."

"Why doesn't she look into her crystal ball

and tell us who the murderer is?" Rage laughed at his own joke.

Katie thought uneasily of Nicole's conviction that Steve was the murderer. She couldn't tell Rage about that. "Maybe it's not so easy," she said. "Maybe the signals aren't too clear."

"I'll bet." He snorted. "I don't believe in any of that junk."

"Well, about Steve—" Katie began.

"Why are you so curious about Steve?" Rage asked. "I thought you two were tight. If you want to know something about him, why don't you ask him yourself?"

"He doesn't like to talk about himself. Haven't you noticed that?"

"Nope."

"Well, maybe it's different with the two of you, but when he's around me, he doesn't talk about himself."

"Maybe there's a reason for that."

"What?" Katie asked quickly.

Rage wrapped up his burger and stuffed it back in the paper bag. "I gotta go."

"No, don't go!" Katie pleaded. "Tell me!"

"I just don't think we ought to be talking about Steve behind his back like this."

Before Katie could stop him, he jumped up and hurried out of the restaurant. She heard his car roaring away outside.

Chapter Thirteen

"Look! Here it is," Tracy said. She and Katie were behind the auditorium building after school. Tracy was looking around as though she expected secret service agents to jump out at any moment. With a self-important air, she slowly pulled open a metal door.

Katie had a momentary fear that there was going to be a body inside and was relieved to see only shelves of window cleaner, heavy-duty detergent, and brushes. A deep utility sink and a few mops sat under the bare bulb that illumined the room. A duffel bag was propped in the corner. She looked at Tracy in confusion. "It's just a storage room."

"Look again," Tracy hissed. "I think the janitor lives here."

Katie's scalp prickled when she saw the cot Tracy was pointing to. A coarse wool blanket was tucked around the mattress and a few terry-cloth towels had been laid at its foot. The cot was so close to the color of its surroundings, a mottled shade of grunge, that it looked as if it had grown in place like a fungus.

"I thought you might want to tell the principal about this place," Tracy said.

"Me? Why don't you tell him?"

Tracy closed the door. "I'm afraid the janitor might find out and go after me because I told on him."

"Don't be silly. How would he ever find out? It's impossible."

"That shows how much you know," Tracy said. "He's sneaking around all the time. It seems like every time I turn around he's standing there watching me. The only reason I was willing to come here now is because I just saw him go over to the football field. Let's get out of here. This place is giving me the creeps."

Katie looked around at the corridor they were standing in. It was no more than a dingy space between the back of the auditorium building and the industrial arts building. Open to the sky, it had a narrow sidewalk and a stairway that led to the unused second floor of the industrial arts building. Tracy was right, Katie thought. It was a creepy place.

The two girls hurried out into the open. Then, breathing a little easier, they walked toward the student parking lot. "It was only by accident that I found his hiding place at all," Tracy continued. "Mrs. Fane asked me to go get a mop for her, and I was already downstairs before I realized I didn't know where they keep the mops. I opened that door to check and I saw that somebody was living there. At first I was going to tell Mrs. Fane, but by the time I got back to class the janitor was already mopping up, so I just got out of there real quick without saying anything. That's when I ran into you."

Katie thought for a moment. "It's no big deal, Tracy. If the janitor really did put that bed in there, all it means is that he's trying to save on his rent. But for all we know it doesn't have anything to do with him. It could have been here for years. The last janitor could have left that stuff there."

The girls stood on the sidewalk by the parking lot. Their classmates shouted greetings to one another as cars pulled out of the lot, spewing exhaust fumes. From the back of the parking lot came the low growling sound of the school buses pulling out.

"If you're so sure about it, why can't you be

the one to report it?" Tracy whined.

"Because you're the one who thinks it's a big deal. You're the one who found it. Why should I report it?" Ever since Katie had seen the yearbook picture of Hugo Clements when he was her age, he had seemed more like a real human being to her. She wasn't as afraid of him, and she felt guilty for having suspected him. It even crossed her mind that it would be a shame for him to lose his job. "Honestly," she said, "I'll bet lots of people take little naps on the job. I mean, they might not want their boss to know, but it doesn't mean they're murderers or anything."

Tracy wilted. "I don't see why you can't do me this teensy little favor."

"Give it up, Tracy. I'm not going to do it. Can I give you a ride home or anything?"

"I guess you could take me to the mall," Tracy said grudgingly.

A black sports car pulled out near them, its spinning wheels spraying Katie's legs with gravel. Glancing up in alarm, Katie saw that it was Steve's car. She wished that he had at least beeped, or shown any sign at all that he had seen her. Logically, Katie knew that he probably just wasn't looking her way. Maybe he had too much on his mind to notice the scenery. Nevertheless, she got behind the wheel of her car feeling as if she had been deliberately snubbed.

"If I hadn't run into you," Tracy was saying, buckling her seat belt, "I would never have had the nerve to go back to that little room. It's too spooky. I must have been out of my mind to go down there looking for a mop. It would be a perfect place for the strangler to jump me."

"He's probably not even around anymore. It's been weeks since anything happened," Katie pointed out, trying to sound braver than she felt. She steered the car out of the lot.

Tracy stared at her in astonishment. "Boy, what does it take to get you scared? A murder a day? I'm terrified practically out of my mind."

"I've decided it was probably a drifter that did it," Katie said firmly. "By now he's a thousand miles away."

"I hope you're right. But don't blame me if that janitor murders somebody else. I tried to get you to turn him in. Why can't the police catch him?" Tracy asked. "I'm sure he did it. He's always hanging around staring at us. I'll bet he's picking out his next victim. If we could get the principal to fire him we could all relax."

"Tracy, that's ridiculous," Katie said. "You're accusing him just because he looks strange—you're trying to start a witch hunt. This job is his only chance to change his life, and you want to get him fired!"

Katie felt better after her outburst, but Tracy just seemed insulted. She kept harping on the subject all the way to the mall, and Katie was relieved when she was able to drop her off at the entrance.

When Tracy was gone, Katie did her best to put all thoughts of the strangler out of her mind. She drove straight to Flakey's on Sunset Avenue. It was as good a place as any to do her homework, she figured. And secretly she hoped that if she kept going there she would run into Rage again. Of course, she saw him three times a week at play practice, but that was no good. She couldn't exactly question him right in front of Steve.

As soon as Tracy stepped into the mall, she felt better. She had always liked the mall's high ceilings and skylights. She liked the ficus trees and the fountains. And she especially liked the ever-present possibility that she might run into someone she knew. In history class, she had learned about the Roman baths where the ancients went to exercise, to be combed and groomed, and to socialize. Tracy thought the Roman baths sounded just like the mall. Only the mall was better, because there you could get ice cream.

Tracy peered into a shop across from the food pavilion. A salesclerk holding a stack of red berets put them down by a pile of T-shirts. Too bad she was not the red-beret type. Catching a glimpse of her rounded silhouette reflected in the shop window, Tracy backed up and walked by the window again, this time being careful to suck in her stomach and straighten her back. She decided to skip the chocolate almond ice cream. She cast a wistful look at the short skirt on the shop dummy. It would be lovely to be able to fit into one of those by summer. Frozen yogurt was the answer. She would just pop across the parking lot and get some. It was a well-known fact that frozen yogurt was healthful and almost calorie-free.

Tracy's eyes shifted nervously. No sign of the janitor so far. She realized she was getting obsessed about him, but she couldn't help it. He was creepy. If she could only get someone else to report his secret hideaway. Maybe Mrs. Fane would tell on the janitor! Mrs. Fane wouldn't be afraid. Tracy's step lightened at the thought. The very first thing tomorrow morning, she decided, she would go in and tell Mrs. Fane what she had found.

She pushed open one of the doors to the mall and stepped outside. Near the doors stood an old lady wearing a long coat. She had hooked her cane over one arm and held her open purse with shaky hands. Tracy turned away from the old lady and headed toward the frozen-yogurt shop across the parking lot. She glanced both ways and noticed a car driving toward her, so she waited until the car slowed slightly before stepping into the drive.

Suddenly, Tracy heard the roar of an engine. She jerked her head up and saw to her horror that the car had speeded up instead of stopping. Tracy tried to jump backward, but it was too late. She was caught by the right fender and swept up onto the hood. The car roared on as Tracy's body landed in a heap at the feet of the astonished old lady.

Tracy lay crumpled on the asphalt, her mouth open. A trickle of blood trailed down her chin.

Chapter Fourteen

Katie had just put her tray down on one of Flakey's front tables when she saw an ambulance speeding down the highway, its siren wailing. After the siren died away she became aware once more of children playing outside and the cheerful refrain, "Welcome to Flakey's. May I take your order?" But the ordinary, comforting sounds of the restaurant could not work their magic on her tonight.

Bryan and Nicole appeared in the doorway, and Nicole immediately ran over to Katie's table. "Did you hear what happened?" she cried. "Tracy's been run down by a hit-and-run driver."

Katie sat in stunned silence while Bryan brought a couple of large drinks to the table. Nicole took two aspirins out of a flat tin in her purse and washed them down with a gulp of soda. "It's awful. I'm getting a migraine."

"Is she okay?" Katie asked.

"We don't know," Nicole told her. "It just happened. She was unconscious when the paramedics got there, but that's all we were able to find out. We were driving by the mall and we saw the ambulance, so we went into the parking lot to check it out. I thought maybe some old person had a heart attack or something. There was a big crowd on the sidewalk. Mike Green had been there ever since the ambulance arrived, and he told us it was Tracy."

"One lady saw it happen, but she's about a hundred years old," Bryan said. "She was so confused she couldn't even remember the color of the car, much less what make it was."

"Mike said Tracy was still breathing when they loaded her into the ambulance," said Nicole. "So far, that's all we know. When we get home I'm going to call the hospital and see if I can find out anything else. I'm so scared. It's like there's a curse on the mall."

"I can't believe this. I just dropped Tracy off there a minute ago," Katie said.

"The guy who hit her just left her there on the pavement." Nicole shook her head. "If she dies, he ought to be charged with murder."

The word hung in the air between them. Murder.

"Of course, this was an accident," Bryan put in hastily. "It's not like it had anything to do with the murders. Whoever hit her must have been drunk. Why else wouldn't he stop?"

Katie leaned toward them urgently. "Tracy had just told me how afraid she was of the janitor. She showed me this storage room where somebody has a cot. She thinks the janitor is living there and she said she wanted to tell the principal. But she was afraid if she did the janitor would get her for it."

"I wish you'd stop this obsession you've got with the janitor," Nicole snapped. "Are you trying to say he ran over Tracy? It's ridiculous. I'll bet he doesn't even know her."

"Maybe. But it's funny that when I saw her she was so afraid of him and then all of a sudden she gets hit by a car."

"Maybe she wasn't looking where she was going," Bryan suggested. "It's happened to me. Sometimes you forget to look both ways if something's really bugging you."

"I'm getting those really bad feelings again," Nicole whispered.

"The voices?" Katie asked anxiously.

Nicole shot her a nasty look. Too late, Katie remembered that Nicole didn't like to talk about her psychic gifts in front of Bryan. She was convinced boys didn't get romantic about girls who could see into the future.

"Just bad feelings," Nicole repeated firmly. "That's all. I tell you, I'm not taking any chances. I'm going straight home and getting in bed. The safest place I can be is under the covers eating a pint of Häagen-Dazs ice cream. That's what I always do when I feel like I'm about to scream."

Katie felt sure it would take more than ice cream to get her mind off what had just happened.

After Nicole and Bryan left, Katie looked out the window for a moment, watching pudgy-legged children shrieking happily as they played. Bryan must be right about what had happened, she decided. Tracy had been too upset to watch where she was going and had stepped right in front of a car.

Katie looked down at her open history book, but she couldn't keep her mind on the reading. She kept thinking that four in the afternoon was an odd time for a drunk driver to be careening through the mall parking lot.

She wasn't sure how long she had been sitting there when Rage came over to her table. "You living at Flakey's now?" he asked, eyebrows raised in surprise. He sat down across from her and began unwrapping his burger. Katie couldn't imagine how he stayed skinny eating those giant burgers. Pink sauce dribbled onto his fingers.

"Tracy just got run down by a hit-and-run driver," Katie said.

Rage put his burger down hastily. "You're kidding me. Is she dead?"

"I don't know. They took her off in an ambulance. I think she was so upset by all these murders that she might have stepped right in front of the car. That's what Bryan thinks."

"Weird." Rage shook his head. "Seems like it's just been one thing after another."

"You're right," Katie said. "Every time I turn around something horrible happens."

"Yeah, it wasn't like this last year. Last year everything was perfect." He smiled. "Hey, I was Malvolio in *Twelfth Night*. Now that was fun. I was practically the star of the show."

"And absolutely nobody that we knew had died." Katie prodded her cold fries with her finger. She glanced up at Rage. "Of course, Steve hadn't moved to town yet, so that's one thing that's better about this year. You must have been glad when he moved here, too, you two being old friends and all."

"Sure."

"What's his family like? I've never even met them." Katie held her breath. She felt she had worked her first question into the conversation very smoothly and was pleased with herself. If only Rage would cooperate.

"They're okay, I guess. I've never met Patton myself, actually."

"But I thought you knew his family real well!"

"Well, I did. Sort of." Rage tugged at one ear and avoided her gaze. "So what did you think of Kingsley's chemistry test?"

Katie glared at him. "Rage, are you trying to keep something from me? Out with it, okay? Is there some kind of big secret about Steve or something?"

"It's no big deal." Rage was still avoiding her eyes.

"Steve wouldn't care if you told me," she wheedled. "You know I'm on his side."

"Why don't you ask him yourself, then?"

"If it's not very important, I don't see why you can't tell me," Katie argued. "What's the problem?"

Rage hesitated. "Mr. Patton's not Steve's father," he said finally. "He's his stepfather. Steve's name used to be Schulemburger, not Patton. It gets me all confused now. I can't get used to it."

"Steve's parents are divorced? Is that all?" Katie leaned back against the padded banquette, feeling more relieved than she would have liked to admit. "Lots of people are divorced. That's nothing."

Rage shrugged.

"Maybe that's why Steve doesn't like to come to Flakey's," Katie said. "Maybe he doesn't get along that well with his stepfather and he doesn't want to help out his restaurant. What was his real father like?"

"Kind of . . ." Rage hesitated. "Well, kind of an alcoholic, actually."

"That's terrible!" Katie cried. "Does he ever get to see his dad? Or is he just pretty much out of the picture?"

Rage began studiously taking his hamburger apart and rearranging it. Finally, he mumbled something Katie couldn't hear.

"What did you say?" She leaned closer.

"I guess you could say he's pretty much out of the picture," he repeated.

"I don't see why this is such a big secret. I mean, everybody understands these days that alcoholism is a disease. Steve would probably feel much better if he talked about it." Katie had the feeling she sounded like Dr. Philpot, but she was sure what she was saying was true nevertheless.

"Maybe I ought to just go ahead and tell you," Rage said in a rush. "Steve's father is in jail for murder. That's why Steve doesn't get to see him. At least, I don't think he does. Unless they have visitors' day or something."

Katie suddenly felt sick.

"You aren't sorry I told you, are you?" Rage asked anxiously. "I guess I shouldn't have. Don't tell Steve I told you, okay?"

Katie gulped. "He's in jail for murder?"

"He killed Steve's stepmother. It happened maybe four years ago. Steve's father and his wife were always fighting and throwing things. That's what I hear, anyway. I guess one night he got carried away. Maybe it was more like an accident. Maybe he wasn't even the one who killed her."

"What does that mean?"

"Look, I don't want to talk about this anymore. I shouldn't have said anything." Rage crumpled the papers on his tray, leaped up, and dumped them into the trash container. "Don't tell Steve I told you, okay?" he said anxiously. Then he fled.

After the shock wore off, Katie tried to figure out her feelings about what Rage had told her. At first it was too confusing. Was she simply hurt that Steve hadn't shared his secret with her? Maybe, but Katie thought there was more to it. After all, she could understand why Steve had kept this to himself. He must have worried that she would break up with him when she found out he was the son of a convict. Maybe she would even think he had inherited his father's homicidal tendencies and be afraid to go out with him.

And he might just be right, Katie thought sadly. She must be afraid that Steve was like his father—why else would she be so upset?

At dinner that night, Katie was scarcely aware of what she was eating. She lifted food to her mouth like a robot.

"Katie?" Mrs. Sloan said.

Katie jumped.

"You're a million miles away. You aren't worried about opening night, are you?" Mr. Sloan asked in a concerned voice.

"Of course she's not worried," Mrs. Sloan said. "She's going to be great. We'll have to get tickets for all our friends so they can see what a beautiful, talented daughter we have."

Katie managed a smile. Somehow opening night had sneaked up on her. She had halfway hoped Mr. Panovitch would delay the play's opening to give her a chance to feel comfortable in her role, but he hadn't suggested it.

"Don't worry, kitten. We know you're going to be a little nervous at first," her father said.

"All great actresses get stage fright," Mrs. Sloan said.

"We're going to let you do your thing opening night without us being there to make you more nervous. We'll come the second or the third night when things have calmed down a little bit. You don't need anything else to worry about."

"Unless you'd like us to be there," Mrs. Sloan chimed in quickly. "If so, you just say the word and we will be."

Katie looked down at her plate and tried to think of the play. "No, I think it would be better if you come the second night." She forced a smile. "At least by then the scenery ought to be dry."

"Don't worry about a thing, you know all your lines perfectly," Mrs. Sloan assured her. "So even if you are a little nervous, you won't forget anything. And all that adrenaline pumping into your bloodstream will just help your performance. Besides, you know you'll do fine with Steve right there next to you."

Katie wondered what her parents would say if she told them Steve's father was a murderer. That would wipe the smiles off their faces, she thought.

Chapter Fifteen

Katie got up early Saturday morning. All night she had tossed and turned, thinking about what Rage had told her. Now she was determined to find out more about it. Rage was obviously very reluctant to talk, and she couldn't even be sure he had his facts straight. But the murder of Steve's stepmother was bound to have been covered in the newspaper. She hoped the library would have the information she was looking for.

Outside, Saturday morning newspapers lay unclaimed in the driveways. Bicycles and Hot Wheels sat silent on porches. It was as if the entire world were asleep. Pushing away thoughts of the strangler, Katie started the car and headed for the library.

When she got there, she was surprised to find the parking lot filled with cars. Mothers with clinging toddlers were bent on the children's room and several students were roaming through the reference room. Katie hoped she wouldn't run into anyone she knew. It would be hard to explain why she was going through newspapers that were four years old.

Katie found the microfilm room and sat at the machine farthest away from the front of the library. That way she would be able to sit for hours without anyone's knowing what she was reading.

She knew that Steve's stepmother had died about four years before. All she had to do was to look through every day's newspaper until she found the murder story. It might take a long time, but it ought to be possible. She recalled reading that more murders took place in the summer because that was when tempers were shortest, so she decided to start with June and go from there.

At least she could understand Steve's air of suppressed sadness now. What could be worse than having his stepmother dead and his father in prison for killing her? No wonder he avoided talking about his past. She mounted the spool of microfilm on the machine and turned on the light. Schulemburger, she reminded herself, was the name she was looking for, not Patton.

As she moved quickly throught the papers, she wondered how Steve's father had felt when Steve had changed his name. Presumably the change had made sense. Steve's hometown, Tyler Falls, was not all that far from Rock Creek, and there must be plenty of people who remembered the murder. Mrs. Patton, Steve's mother, had probably thought a story like that wasn't good for her image.

Katie's progress on the microfilm was achingly slow. The work was so monotonous that after a while she scarcely noticed the pages as they sped by before her eyes. Special offers and sales of long ago appeared, together with blurred photographs of brides and the winners of spelling bees. Suddenly her hand froze and the microfilm wheel stopped its squeaking progress. "Wife of Bank President Slain," read the headline on the screen. What had caught her eye was the name in small type—Schulemburger.

A quick scan of the story confirmed that this was what she was looking for. It recounted that Stephen Schulemburger had found his wife dead when he returned from a walk late one summer evening. In his statement to the police, he said he had not realized she was dead at first and had tried to revive her before calling the rescue squad.

Katie could have guessed even from the brief newspaper account that Steve's father was going to be the police's prime suspect. Didn't they always suspect the husband? Leafing ahead only a few days, she found the story of his arrest. This time the paper printed a large picture of the Schulemburger family "in happier days." Steve looked happier and round-faced. His younger sister Jenny looked maybe eight or ten, and a handsome Irish setter sat at the feet of his pretty young stepmother. Stephen Schulemburger, tall and broad-shouldered, looked a lot like Steve.

A breath of cool air brushed Katie's face. When she looked up, she saw Nicole staggering in the front door of the library with an armful of books. Katie hunched over the microfilm screen, hoping to be inconspicuous, but it was no use. Nicole had spotted her and hurried straight to the microfilm machine.

"Katie? I thought you always slept late on Saturday. What are you doing working?" Nicole perched on the table next to the microfilm machine. "Can you believe the mall still hasn't gotten that new shipment of Cliffs Notes? I'm desperate. I've been skipping the reading because I thought I'd catch up when the Cliffs Notes came in. Now that I'm hopelessly behind, all of a sudden we've got this test! I could kill Mr. P. I just hope the library has a copy. You haven't beat me to it, have you?"

"No," Katie said, "I'm not looking for Cliffs Notes. I've been keeping up with the reading, more or less. Did you ever find out anything about Tracy? You said you were going to call the hospital."

"I did," Nicole said grimly. "They airlifted her to the trauma unit. Then I called this cousin of my mom's who works in the hospital. She told me that the police weren't able to find out anything from Tracy about what happened because she got a bad blow on the head. And her neck is broken so they've got her heavily sedated to keep her from thrashing around and doing her spinal cord any damage. They have to keep her zonked out until they can get her into a neck brace, which will be days. They won't know if she's really going to be all right until they take her out from under the sedation and see whether she can talk and everything."

"Her neck was broken?" Katie gulped. "Of course, it was just an accident. It's not at all like the other times."

Nicole looked sober. "Katie, there's something I need to tell you about the car that hit her. I think—" Suddenly her eye was caught by the photograph of Steve's family. "Hey, that guy in the picture looks like Steve!"

Katie switched off the light in the microfilm machine and the screen went blank. "Nicole, we've got to talk."

Nicole grabbed a nearby chair and pulled it up to Katie's, sitting so they were knee to knee. "I know we do. That's what I was just about to say. But you go first. Is it about Steve?"

"Steve's dad is in jail."

Nicole's eyes went blank with surprise. "Since when? What was it, embezzling? Why wasn't it in the paper? With Harvey Patton such a big deal around here, I'd think it would be all over. Did it just happen?"

"Harvey Patton isn't Steve's real father. It's his real father who's in jail. For murder."

"Oh, my God," breathed Nicole.

"I'm actually kind of hurt that Steve didn't tell me." Katie looked down and aimlessly unbuckled and buckled the strap of her watch. "I found out about it only yesterday. Rage told me that his father killed Steve's stepmother. I've just been looking up the old newspaper stories trying to find out more. "

"How terrible!"

"He strangled her."

Wordlessly, Nicole reached over and switched on the light in the microfilm machine. Instantly, the photograph of Steve's family was projected onto the flat plastic disk of the machine. Nicole's eyes scanned the caption and then she moved the lever to read the rest of the story at the bottom of the page.

"Are you going to tell him you know?" Nicole asked.

Katie hesitated. "Maybe I'll try to get him to tell me first. I'd try to be subtle, of course. I don't want him to know I've been asking Rage about him."

"Good idea. Look, Katie." Nicole licked her lips. "I think maybe you'd better not let him know that you've found out."

"Hi, girls."

Katie wheeled around in her chair and found herself looking up at the janitor. She recoiled when he rested his hairy hand on the back of her chair. "What's up?" he asked. "Any more news about the murders?"

"We only know what we read in the papers," said Nicole. "What about you?"

"Same here," he said. "Same here. Yep, it's the same with me."

Katie switched off the light in the microfilm machine and began rewinding the spool, taking care to avoid looking at the janitor.

"Well," he said, after a moment's silence. "Let me know if you find out anything. We need to get that murderer safe in jail, yes, siree. Nice seeing you. Uh, don't take any wooden nickels." Looking ill at ease, he strode out of the library.

"Don't take any wooden nickels?" Katie repeated incredulously. "How much do you think he heard?"

"Oh, I don't think he was listening. He's lonely, so he came over to say hello."

"What's he even doing here? It's not like he has to work on a research paper."

"He probably comes in to read the newspaper. He can read, you know."

"I guess." Katie took the microfilm off the machine and put it back in its box. "Steve and I are going out tonight."

"Alone? Just the two of you?" Nicole stared at her. "I wonder if that's a good idea."

Katie met her eyes. "Are you still hearing those voices, Nic? What are they saying?"

Nicole shrugged. "I can't tell, but I really have a bad feeling about Steve. I don't think you should be alone with him."

"How can I draw him out and get him to tell me about his father unless we're alone? It's not like he's going to announce it over the school loudspeaker. Nicole, you keep talking about voices, but you can't even hear what they're saying. I can't listen to voices in your head."

Nicole's voice sank to a whisper. "Okay, but don't laugh. When I was on the phone talking to my aunt about Tracy, I got this vision of a black car. I'm sure the car that hit Tracy was black!"

"A black car? Steve's car?" Katie felt herself go cold.

"Black—that's all I could tell." Nicole frowned. "I don't know. It's vague, but awful. Like I was picking up this fear—not Tracy's fear, but the driver's. I know it sounds crazy. I don't know what it means, but I really wish you wouldn't go out with Steve. It's not safe."

Katie shook her head. "I've got to talk to him, Nic. I owe him that. I've got to give him a chance to explain."

Chapter Sixteen

When Steve came to pick up Katie that night, Mr. Sloan switched on the floodlights and watched until they were in the car.

"Your dad is awfully on edge, isn't he?" Steve asked. "I don't remember him doing that before."

"He wants me to stay home all the time until they catch the strangler. But I told him I'd be okay as long as I was with you." Katie darted a glance at Steve.

"So, what movie do you want to see?" Steve asked. "If we go to the mall we can grab a bite at the food court and we'll have a choice of three movies. That way we don't have to make up our minds until we get there."

"I don't think I want to go to a movie. Let's

go someplace where we can get a real meal." Katie knew she couldn't draw Steve out about his father if they were only grabbing a quick hamburger before the movie. "I'll pay half," she added.

"Don't be stupid," he said. "I'm not that hard up."

"How about pizza?"

"You're sure you don't want to see a movie?"

"Too much violence and blood. I've had enough of that in real life."

"Okay." Steve shrugged. "Incidentally," he said, "I've gotten nowhere trying to find out about the police investigation. When I finally tracked down Darren Scott, he told me his mother works at Flakey's now—and he looked at me pretty funny."

"Steve, why don't you ever go to Flakey's?"

"I told you, I get enough of Flakey's at home. It's Flakey's this, Flakey's that, twenty-four hours a day."

"But aren't you proud of what your dad has done? I mean, being chairman of the board and everything?"

His face froze. "You want to go to Flakey's? We can do that. I just thought you wanted pizza, that's all."

"Pizza is fine."

He's not going to tell me, Katie thought

bleakly. It's like I don't even rate as a friend. I'm just somebody he goes out with. She wished she had not persuaded Rage to tell her Steve's secret. Now it lay heavily on her heart and there was nothing she could do about it.

At the Pizza Inn, they took a booth in the corner, right next to the windows. Even though the window only looked on the parking lot, Katie liked to be where she could see outside. She had been feeling so trapped lately.

Steve gave the waitress their order. A moment later she appeared with a tray and placed two plastic glasses of cola in front of them. Then, looking harassed, she darted away.

"Tell me what it was like growing up in Tyler Falls," Katie said.

"It's not worth talking about."

"But you never tell me anything about yourself," she protested.

"It's a boring subject. Look, you're not going to get all weird and start psychoanalyzing me, are you? Because I just can't take it right now. My life is complicated enough."

She squeezed his hand, feeling his warmth, wondering why her own hand was so cold. "What's so complicated about your life?"

"Just—things." He let go of her hand and frowned out the darkened window.

"How can I understand if you never explain

anything to me?" Katie asked gently.

"Don't nag me, Katie. Can't we just have a few laughs and not get into all this junk about my life?"

"I haven't been laughing much lately. And neither have you."

"We can fix that." He smiled. "This man calls a friend's house and a little boy answers the phone—"

"I'm just not in the mood for jokes, Steve."

"I must be telling it wrong. Want to hear some music?"

Before Katie could protest, Steve leaped up and went over to the jukebox. A moment later electric music shot through the room, mingling with the sounds of chatter and the clunk of plastic dishes. When Steve returned and sat down, Katie longed to blurt out "I know all about your father," but she couldn't. For one thing, it would put Rage on the spot for telling her. And she wasn't sure how Steve would take it. He might get pretty upset when he found out she had been asking Rage about him.

The long silence between them was punctuated by the throbbing beat of the music. Katie didn't see how she could go on like this, knowing about his father and not being able to talk about it.

"An angel is passing," Steve said, smiling.

"That's what my grandmother used to say when everybody stops talking at once. Maybe it's kind of wishful thinking, huh? There don't seem to be many angels around these days, judging from recent events."

"Steve, are you keeping something from me?" Katie blurted out.

He looked at her blankly for a moment. "No. At least nothing important. I mean, it doesn't have anything to do with you and me."

Their waitress reappeared and placed the pizza on its stainless steel pedestal. "Pepperoni and mushrooms," she announced.

When she had left, Steve spoke reluctantly. "Okay, maybe we should talk." He hesitated. "But I just don't know where to start."

"Try the beginning."

He smiled. "It was a dark and stormy night—"

"No, really. Tell me what's going on."

"Okay. Let's start with this." He frowned. "Harvey Patton is not my real father. My real father is Stephen Schulemburger. He used to be the president of a bank in Tyler Falls. In fact, he was the youngest bank president United Planters Bank ever had."

Steve hesitated, and Katie knew he was nerving himself for what he had to say. "He and my mom split when I was twelve. I felt like it was the end of the world, but I was wrong. The end of the world came later. Dad married his secretary, which I guess was what he had in mind all along. Personally, I hated her, but Dad had this crazy idea that we were going to love her for breaking up our family. Anyway, then Mom married Patton. He's pretty awful, to tell you the truth. He's got a big belly and he thinks he's God's gift to the system of free enterprise. So as far as I was concerned my life couldn't have been worse. But it got worse. Am I boring you?" He looked at her as if he wished she would say yes, but she shook her head.

"Well," he continued, "skipping all the stuff about how we weren't one big happy family, I guess I'd better just cut to the disaster. One night Dad came home and found my stepmother dead. She'd been strangled."

"No!" Katie hoped she looked genuinely shocked and surprised. Luckily Steve didn't seem aware of her reaction. His eyes had taken on a faraway look, as if he were watching the story unfold on a movie screen only he could see.

"The upshot was they arrested Dad for it and he's at Central Prison right now. That's why I couldn't give you a ride home the other day. I was going to see him. Mom doesn't like it, but she can't stop me now that I've got my license. Every other week I drive up for visitors' day. It's really depressing. I mean, just to get into the visiting room a guard has to let you through all these big clanking doors and if you need to use the bathroom, the guard's got to come back and let you through three more locked gates. Dad's lost thirty pounds, he's getting gray, and he talks real slow. It's like he's fading away right in front of me. And the worst part is—he's innocent, Katie."

"How—how do you know?"

"Because he told me so. He swore to me that he didn't do it." Steve banged his fist on the table and Katie jumped. She could feel her face turning pink. She hoped none of the people nearby were listening to their converstaion.

"Well," Steve said, "there it is. You said you wanted to know about my life."

Katie gulped. "I do."

"You can imagine how I love hearing what a great system of law and order we have when my own father's in prison for something he didn't do."

Katie spoke hesitantly. "But—isn't it hard to send somebody like a bank president to jail unless there's really good evidence?"

She regretted the words as soon as they were out of her mouth.

"They always suspect the husband," Steve said tensely. "But it couldn't have been Dad. He could never have strangled Judy."

"He had never—hit her or anything?"

He shrugged that off. "Okay, maybe they had their troubles. That was one of the things the prosecution made a big deal out of at the trial. But to hit somebody in the middle of an argument isn't the same thing as killing them. They brought in all these X rays of when she broke her jaw a year or so before she died, but the fact is she had slipped in the kitchen. She told me so herself."

Katie had never heard of anybody breaking their jaw by slipping in the kitchen, but she didn't think it would be helpful to point that out to Steve. He obviously needed to believe that his father was innocent.

"The problem is," Steve went on, his voice growing heavy, "Dad didn't have any alibi. He'd been drinking that night. He and Judy had a fight and he went out for a walk to cool off. It looked bad for him, because it was obvious that nobody had broken into the house. Dad told the police that the back door was unlocked when he came in. And the dog was still sleeping out by the garage as if nothing had happened. So the cops figured Dad let himself in with his key and that's why the dog didn't bark."

"It had to be somebody she knew, Steve. If they didn't have a key, she must have let them in. And the dog—"

"I don't know how much you know about Irish setters, Katie, but they aren't the geniuses of the dog world. I don't think the stuff about the dog not barking means a thing. And heck, everybody forgets to lock the back door some time or another. It's obvious that some prowler did it and Dad got stuck with the rap. Can you imagine how helpless it all makes me feel?"

Again, Steve pounded his fist on the table. Frightened by the violence of his gesture, Katie drew away. "I'm so sorry," she whispered.

"Now do you see why I was interested in these murders? We're only thirty miles from my old town, and suddenly girls are getting strangled with a cord, just the way Judy was strangled. It could be her murderer up to his old tricks."

"Isn't that kind of a long shot?" she ventured.

"Maybe, but long shots are all I've got."

Chapter Seventeen

For the first time in weeks, Katie felt as if she understood Steve. His interest in the murders made sense if he hoped this was his chance to clear his father. Katie thought he was grasping at straws, but it was a relief to know there was some logical explanation for his strange reaction to Millicent's and Laurie's deaths.

When Nicole came over Sunday afternoon to study for the *Macbeth* test, Katie filled her in on what she had learned.

"That's grotesque!" breathed Nicole. "I can't believe I thought Steve was so glamorous and rich and everything and he's going over to the prison all the time to visit his dad."

"It explains why Steve has been acting so weird, anyway."

"Wait a minute!" Nicole's eyes opened wide. "Have you thought about this? Maybe Steve *knows* his dad is innocent. Maybe he feels guilty because *he* murdered his stepmother!"

"Don't be ridiculous!" Katie cried.

"Just listen to me, Katie," Nicole said. "Who would his dad be willing to take the rap for? Only Steve. Maybe he knew Steve did it and went to jail to protect him. Little does he know that while he's in prison Steve is continuing his life of crime. He discovered he likes strangling people and now he's at it again."

Katie jumped up. "I've never heard such a bunch of junk in my life. Steve was only twelve or thirteen when his stepmother was murdered."

"Yeah, but he's a big guy. I'll bet he wasn't exactly small even when he was twelve. It looked to me like his stepmother was a tiny woman, so it would have been easy for him. And," Nicole lowered her voice meaningfully, "didn't he tell you himself that he hated her?"

"Lots of people don't like their stepmothers. You're jumping to too many conclusions. I know Steve. I just don't believe he's a serial killer," Katie said as she paced the room. She was uncomfortably aware of how weak her objections sounded.

"How well do you really know him?" Nicole pressed. "You just met him a couple of months ago. You told me that he never talks about himself and you've never met his family. You didn't even know about his father!" she finished triumphantly.

"Why would Steve murder his stepmother and wait four years before he did it again?" Katie asked stubbornly. "Answer that one."

"We don't know for sure that he waited, do we? Maybe he murdered lots of other people before he came here. It's possible."

"You just don't like him. That's the only reason you've come up with this crazy theory," Katie said.

"Not true," said Nicole. "I've sensed there was something wrong with Steve from the beginning, that's all. I knew right off he had a blue aura and that he had all kinds of secrets."

Katie snorted derisively. "Right. I forgot about the aura. That's really great evidence, Nicole."

"It's one kind of evidence," said Nicole with dignity, "and now we're looking at another kind. Just see what's right in front of your face, Katie. Use your brain."

"This is stupid," Katie insisted. "There's no more evidence against Steve than against any other guy you could name."

"We didn't have a single murder until he showed up."

"We didn't have any murders until the janitor came, either," Katie pointed out.

"You've got an obsession about the janitor, you know that?"

"I'm just saying that he's as likely a suspect as Steve. You've got an obsession about Steve!" Katie yelled.

"Maybe. But if I were you, I wouldn't go out with Steve until they round up this murderer. You could be taking a big chance."

"I'm not going to talk about this anymore," Katie said, resolutely opening her book. "Do you want to study or not?"

Nicole obediently dropped the subject, but Katie knew that her friend wasn't about to give up her suspicions. Worst of all, Katie found herself thinking about Nicole's absurd theory.

If only the police would catch the real murderer! Katie thought. But the newspapers had not mentioned the investigation in days.

When Steve got to rehearsal Wednesday afternoon, he saw a group of kids gathered around Nicole.

"What's up?" he asked Katie.

"Tracy's regained consciousness," she told him excitedly.

"She can talk," Nicole was saying, "and they say she's okay except for her broken neck.

They're going to put her in this halo-type brace. She could be back in school in a couple of weeks if everything goes right."

"Could she describe the car that hit her?" Steve asked.

"She can't remember a thing. I hear that happens lots of times with severe concussions. The cops went to the trauma center to question her, but she didn't even know that a car had hit her, much less what kind of car it was."

Mr. Panovitch interrupted the group. "Pick up your brooms, people," he cried. "Sweep those floors."

"Why do we have to sweep the floors all of a sudden?" Rage whined. "I thought we were artistes, not slaves."

Mike Green snapped a bit of straw off a broom and began sucking on it loudly. "I hear the janitor quit. That's why we have to sweep. Next it's going to be scrubbing toilets."

"Why did he quit?" Steve asked.

"He was asked to take over General Motors, I bet," Mike quipped.

"Those brooms aren't just for show!" Mr. Panovitch screeched. "Use them, people. We don't want our opening-night crowd to think we're pigs."

Steve followed Katie to one corner of the stage. He wanted a chance to talk to her alone so he could thank her for listening to him the other night. He had been surprised at how good it felt to finally get his secret out in the open.

Things had been bad in his hometown after his father's conviction. He knew that people were always whispering behind his back. But to his surprise he had felt even worse after he moved to Rock Creek. In Rock Creek no one knew about his father. No one even knew his real name. But the weird thing was that all of a sudden he didn't feel like himself anymore. The Steve Patton who had the fancy car and lived in the big white house was somebody he didn't even know.

He had started going to visit his father at the prison as soon as he got his license, and the visits gave his life an even stranger quality. It was hard to fit together the days when he saw his father with the more ordinary days when he spent his time taking out the garbage, driving his sister to piano lessons, and doing his homework.

When he was at the prison, he felt a constant twisting in his gut. Neither he nor his father knew what to say. They stared at each other in silence for long minutes. The injustice of Mr. Schulemburger's imprisonment weighed on them both, making it hard even to breathe. Driving home, Steve always thought bitterly about "the land of the free and the home of the brave." His world was split in half—the normal and the bizarre. School and jail.

And his mother had been cool toward him ever since he had begun the visits. She wanted to pretend his father had never existed. Lots of people in Rock Creek assumed Harvey Patton was Steve's real father, and his mother liked it that way. But Steve hated it. He wanted his old identity back, even if it hurt. Katie was the first person he could talk to about himself, and he wanted to make sure she knew how important that was to him.

Katie was happy when Mr. Panovitch said they could stop sweeping and start rehearsing. Steve had been talking to her about his father ever since rehearsal started, and she was getting uncomfortable. She couldn't help thinking that she had been happier before she knew about Steve's father. Everything seemed different now. All she really knew about Steve, she had realized belatedly, was that he was handsome, drove a fancy car, and was a good actor. Was Nicole right? Was she taking a chance even to go out with him?

Mr. Panovitch's voice cut through her thoughts. "Remember!" he cried. "Friday is dress rehearsal and Saturday is opening night!"

Katie gulped. She was all too aware that although she had her lines memorized, she wasn't exactly wonderful in the part. So much had happened that it had been hard to give her full attention to being a convincing leprechaun.

"I want magnificence," screamed Mr. Panovitch. "Not mere competence. I want that audience shouting 'Bravo!'"

"I just want to get through the performance," Katie said. How would she ever project her modest singing voice?

It was the worst rehearsal yet. Many cues were missed and members of the chorus kept tripping all over each other.

"Don't worry," cried Mr. Panovitch. "It'll be all right on The Night. Remember, this has to be a team effort. We are creating a world of lightness and fantasy."

Mr. Panovitch was still gathering steam when Steve tugged at Katie's sleeve, signaling that he was ready to go.

"I hope we're not missing anything important," Katie said when they were outside.

"We're not," said Steve. "Trust me."

Trust me. The words echoed in Katie's brain. Of course she trusted him. She just wished she could stop thinking about what Nicole had said.

The air was chilly as they walked through the parking lot. Steve unlocked the door of his black Corvette. "Know what this is?" he said.

"It's a bribe. Harvey Patton gave it to me when I turned sixteen. I guess it was supposed to make me forget my dad. It didn't work."

Katie let her fingers slide across the smooth black surface of the door as she got in the car. She didn't know what to say to Steve anymore. She couldn't stop feeling afraid of him.

Steve reached over and touched her knee lightly. "It was a pretty rotten rehearsal, wasn't it?"

"I wonder if it's ever going to come together. We seem to be getting worse instead of better."

"It always looks that way," said Steve. "But when that adrenaline starts pumping, everything runs smooth as silk."

He pulled the car out of the lot and soon they were driving through the streets of town. As they whizzed along, Katie felt almost dizzy. Bars of shadows flickered briefly across her vision.

"I'm so happy I don't have to hide anything from you anymore," said Steve. "It was awful having to pretend everything was just great when my insides were churning like mad."

Katie smiled weakly. Steve looked so much like his father that it was spooky. And watching his large hands gripping the steering wheel made her vaguely uneasy.

Luckily, he did not notice her silence. "What

I'm really afraid of now," he said, "is that the investigation of the murders will just die down."

"They never close a murder case."

"Maybe not officially. But if there isn't any new evidence, it stands to reason the police don't keep working on it twenty-four hours a day. I just wish something else would happen."

"Steve! You don't mean you want another murder!"

"It would be a change, anyway," said Steve.

She looked at him in alarm.

"You don't have to act like I'm beating up on old ladies, Katie. Of course I don't want another murder. I just want the murderer to make some mistake."

"How can he do that unless he kills again?" Katie asked.

"Don't put words in my mouth," he snapped.

"Well, how else could it happen?" she pressed.

"He could confess! How about that?"

"Somehow," Katie said slowly, "I don't think he's going to."

"I don't know what I think. I can't believe that somebody would strangle two girls in two weeks and then give it up. Don't you have a feeling that something has got to happen? It's like it's time for act three."

Act III, enter the murderer, Katie thought. It

was as if he were a shadowy figure, waiting in the wings for his cue. Was Nicole right? Was Katie herself going to be the next victim? Her gaze was drawn to Steve's face—but she couldn't read his expression. In the uncertain light of the car, his eyes looked strangely empty.

Chapter Eighteen

"Are you leaving already?" Mrs. Sloan asked.

Katie checked her lipstick in the mirror over the mantel. "I want to be there early. I'm nervous enough without having to worry about something making me late."

"You'll be early to your own funeral."

Katie winced. She wished her mother had put it another way. Worrying about the play was bad enough without being reminded of funerals. "I just hope my voice is okay," she said. "I've been trying not to talk much."

"Don't worry," said Mrs. Sloan. "You're going to be great!" Mr. Sloan peered out the window. "Maybe I'll just drive you over there."

"Dad! It's not dark yet, and I'm only going to school. It's going to be swarming with people.

What I'm scared of is forgetting my lines." Katie clutched her stomach at the thought. "You'll have the prompter to help you if you get stuck," Mrs. Sloan said. "Not that you'll need one. You'll be perfect."

"Remember, kitten, it's only a play." Her father kissed her on the forehead. "And you're always our little star no matter what happens."

Katie winced again. Her parents were obviously as nervous as she was. She was glad they weren't going with her to opening night. The last thing she needed was them standing in the wings trying to build up her self-confidence.

"I could do the play in my sleep," she said aloud. "I've practiced and practiced." She grabbed her dog-eared copy of the script and headed for the door.

"Wouldn't you like a glass of orange juice before you leave?" Mrs. Sloan asked. "For extra energy."

"No!" Katie bounded out the door. When she reached the car and looked up, she saw her father standing at the door watching her.

"Jeez," she muttered feelingly. "No wonder I'm a nervous wreck!"

Katie knew she hadn't put in enough time on the play. It just hadn't seemed very important. All of a sudden she wished she had worked on it more. But it was too late now.

Driving out of the neighborhood, she reached over to touch the script, as if she could somehow absorb the words through her fingertips. The scene she was shakiest on was the one with the jig. Once she got to school, she thought, she might even walk it through on the stage, unless the stagehands and the chorus were all over the place. Self-confidence was what she needed.

Katie turned the car onto Eastern Avenue. Dusk gave a somber tone to the streets, and the streetlights didn't help. It would be nice to arrive at the brightly lit auditorium and meet up with all the other kids.

When Katie pulled into the student parking lot, she saw that, as usual, she was the first cast member to arrive. Mr. Panovitch's old blue sedan was parked in one of the teachers' places near the circular drive, so at least the building would be open. Katie gathered up the pages of her script and hesitated. She wasn't sure she really wanted to be alone in the auditorium with Mr. Panovitch. Ever since his stunt with the doll she had felt uncomfortable around him. Katie's glance flitted nervously over the building complex. Don't be silly, she told herself. Who do you expect to see? A lurking murderer? The janitor?

Her heart was pounding. I need to calm

down, she thought. Katie was nervous about the play, but she knew it wasn't just that. She had been jumpy for weeks, ever since Millicent's death.

Then she saw Rage approaching. Almost absurdly relieved, Katie got out of the car and waved to him.

"Where did you park?" she called, glancing around at the empty parking lot.

"On the other side. I figured there's going to be a mob here tonight. We'll be running out of parking places."

Rage's hands were thrust determinedly into his pockets as if to keep himself from fidgeting. He's as keyed up as I am, she realized. And he's only singing in the chorus. Mom must be right about everyone being nervous before a performance.

"I see you're here early, as usual," he said.

"I always think the car is going to break down or something. I don't know why. I've never had a flat tire, but I always think I'm going to get one."

Katie glanced uneasily toward the auditorium. In a burst of landscaping enthusiasm, the builders had clustered masses of bushes and trees on either side of the sloped building. Katie had always rather admired the way it looked from the road, but in her present state of mind, heavy foliage seemed a likely place for a murderer to lurk. She was glad Rage was there.

As they drew close to the building, Rage veered to the left. "Let's go around the back way," he said.

"Why?" Katie asked. "It's farther. We'll have to go all the way around the building."

"I want to show you something."

Katie wondered if Rage knew about the janitor's little hiding place. Curiously, she followed him to the back of the building. As Katie stepped into the alley between the auditorium and the industrial arts building, she felt warm hands encircle her throat. Shocked, she tried to scream, but the pressure on her throat prevented her from making a sound.

She was aware of a ballooning blackness in her brain just before she lost consciousness.

Ten minutes later, Steve watched as Nicole got out of her car in the student parking lot holding her freshly ironed costume aloft on a hanger.

Steve slammed his car door shut and frowned at the auditorium building. He had expected to see Katie's car parked in the lot. "Nicole, where's Katie?"

"Probably back at her house throwing up," Nicole said. "I've never seen such a bad case of stage fright. Didn't you notice that she didn't eat at lunch?"

Now that Nicole mentioned it, Steve remembered that Katie had been nervous. He wished he had given her a call to reassure her. The problem was that acting didn't come as easily to her as it did to the rest of them. But Steve knew that didn't matter. All that mattered was that she was pretty and she could sing. She was getting herself all worked up over nothing. Still, he thought, she should be here by now.

People drifted toward the auditorium and cast members kept arriving. Every time Steve heard a car, he spun around, hoping that this time it would be Katie. He wished he had gone by to pick her up. All of a sudden he realized he didn't like the idea of her driving alone. He stood in the parking lot and watched anxiously for her.

Mike rested his hand on Steve's shoulder. "Ah, life!" he cried. "I cannot hold thee close enough."

"Get your hands off me," Steve snarled.

"Sheesh." Mike recoiled. "What have we got here? Oscar the Grouch?"

"You can touch me anytime you want, Mike," a sophomore girl simpered.

"Sure thing." Mike threw his arm around the skinny blonde and winked.

Ignoring them, Steve plodded toward the auditorium, his head down. He knew what was bothering him. He had been halfway hoping that another murder would occur, one that would give the police a lead. Now, with a superstitious dread, he wondered if he was going to be punished for the wish. If something had happened to Katie, he would never forgive himself. She was the only person in town that he'd allowed himself to care about.

He had felt better ever since he told Katie the truth. She wasn't one of those girls who were only interested in his car. There was something warm and generous about her that made him certain she wouldn't back away from the hard truth he had to tell. She hadn't disappointed him. In fact, she hadn't even seemed surprised—it was as if she already knew. Something important had clicked into place that night, a rush of warmth he had never felt before. He didn't want to lose her now.

Chapter Nineteen

When Katie opened her eyes, she was overcome by nausea. She couldn't move her arms or her legs. She was cramped uncomfortably and her head hurt. One of her feet was cold—she must have lost a shoe. When her vision cleared, she caught a dizzying view of the sidewalk. Something was hurting her mouth, she realized dimly. She couldn't move her tongue.

The cable knit of Rage's black turtleneck was only inches from her eyes, and she could smell the saddle soap he used on his leather pants. The ridge of his shoulder bit into her belly and her head bumped sharply against his back. Slowly her brain cleared and the disjointed sensations began to make sense. She realized that Rage had tied her hands and feet and slung her over his shoulder. Her mouth and tongue were hurt by a gag wedged tightly between her teeth. She could feel it biting into her cheeks. Furious, she bit down on the dirty gag, tasting the linty cotton. Having her tongue trapped gave her the panicky feeling that she might choke.

With a sudden effort she tried to straighten her body, hoping to wrest her way free. She was rewarded with a burning pain in her thigh. Her eyes stung with tears of indignation as she realized that Rage had bitten her. "Don't try anything," he growled. "That's only a sample of what you're going to get if you don't keep still."

Katie's ears buzzed, and she felt faintness threatening her. No one would know what had become of her, she thought miserably. She would disappear without a trace. She sensed the presence of looming buildings on either side of them, blocking the light. My car! she thought suddenly. The police would find her car. But that hope quickly disappeared. With a dead certainty she knew Rage would move her car.

She clenched her hands tightly until her nails bit sharply into her palms. The pain was good because it was something she could control, her only remaining bit of freedom. She thought of Steve's wish that the murderer would make a mistake, leave a trail for the police. At least she could try to leave some sign that she had been here. Straining, she forced her nails into the soft flesh of her palm. At last she felt the stickiness of her own blood. Struggling frantically as Rage kicked open a metal door, she tried to touch the doorjamb with her blood-damp hand. She felt the metal briefly under her palm, but she couldn't tell whether she had managed to get any blood on it. Her head banged against the metal door, and Rage threw her roughly to the cement floor inside the room. She fell against a heavy porcelain sink, hitting her head again.

Nausea broke over her like a wave. Struggling to swallow, she blinked away tears. The gag bit into the soft flesh of her mouth. Her tongue seemed to trap her breath in her throat, and she felt herself choking. Fighting against panic, she pushed her tongue hard against the gag and gasped for breath. She knew she had to be calm or she would choke again. Breathing was all that mattered now.

Slowly she became conscious of the smooth feel of cold metal. Her bare foot was jammed against the leg of a cot. She realized that she was in the janitor's room at the back of the auditorium building. The entire drama club must be agonizingly close by. Suddenly she felt fingers in her hair and a wrenching pain as Rage jerked her head around to face him. "Are you afraid?"

he whispered. "You should be, because I'm going to hurt you."

Katie shrank from him, her stomach clenched with fear. A single damp lock of Rage's hair fell into his face. She saw his eyes with a clarity that dismayed her. She was appalled by the pleasure she saw there. The sour smell of the mop beside the sink filled her nostrils and a sharp ticking sound like an old-fashioned alarm clock seemed to echo mockingly inside her skull.

"I guess you thought I wasn't good enough for you," Rage whispered. "You had to have Steve with his fancy car and his jokes and his stupid grin. I bet you're sorry now."

Katie wondered if she could tell Rage that she liked him. She knew she was no actress, but to save her life . . . No, she told herself firmly. If by some miracle he removed the gag, she would scream.

Suddenly he let go of her hair and stood up. "Steve always had everything. But now he's got a jailbird father and pretty soon he's going to have a dead girlfriend. And you know who they're going to suspect? Him!" He laughed softly. "They always suspect the boyfriend. I've got it all worked out. This is going to be perfect. My best yet. I'm really an artiste, you know. An artiste of pain." His face contorted suddenly.

Katie scarcely felt the blow as his boot struck her. Her palms and feet were tingling with adrenaline. She could bear anything if only he didn't kill her.

He's insane, she thought. When he bent over her the muscles in her neck tensed. She felt herself grow weak with fear.

"Are you afraid?" he asked softly. Apparently what he saw in her eyes satisfied him, because he stepped back from her and chuckled.

Katie strained at her bonds. The cords bit into her flesh, and she realized with a sinking heart that she was tied fast.

"You thought I was going to strangle you just now, didn't you?" Rage said softly. "I do like to strangle girls. It's fun."

The calm pleasure in his voice made her go rigid with horror.

"Steve's stepmother, Judy, was my first," he continued pleasantly. "I don't think she ever knew what happened. Too bad, because it's more fun when they're really scared. Like you are."

It was so hard for her to swallow. She realized that he must have stuffed a loose wedge of material in behind the gag. She frantically pushed at the material with her tongue.

Rage stretched a length of cord between his hands, wrapped it around one hand, and snapped it. She couldn't take her eyes off his hands after that. Horrified, she wondered if she would feel anything when he killed her.

"I got this cord at a garage sale when I was a kid," he said in a conversational tone. "A big spool of it. I took some of it over to Steve's house the night I killed Judy. He said I could borrow his old stilts, and I was thinking I would tie them onto my bicycle to take home. When I went inside the house, I could tell Judy'd been crying and she didn't want me to see how puffy her eyes were." He smiled.

"She had real short hair, and when she turned around the light from the overhead lamp was on her long white neck. It was like some long-stemmed lily. She shouldn't have bent over like that if she didn't want to be strangled, you know? She was tempting me. I looped the cord around her neck and pulled it real tight, and in no time at all she was crumpled on the floor. I kept thinking she was going to get up. It didn't seem possible she was dead. I hadn't meant to do it, but she made it too easy. I knew I was really going to be in big trouble if anybody found out. My mom would have killed me—she's got a bad temper. I thought, boy, I'll never do *this* again. But I wanted to remember it, you know? Because it was kind of special. I had this little camera in my pocket—I was really into taking pictures then—so I just took a quick shot, like a souvenir, and then I got out of there." He flexed the cord.

"I was kind of surprised when they thought Steve's dad did it. But Mr. Schulemburger had hit her lots of times—that's what it said in the paper. It was just a technicality that I happened to kill her before he did. And the look on Steve's face when they came to get his father—it was priceless. It knocked him flat. After that happened, kids just didn't want to be around him much anymore. He knew then what it felt like to be treated like dirt." Rage's face hardened.

"I hated it when he showed up here, making me feel little and ugly all over again. Everybody was acting like he was hot stuff, like he was the crown prince of the universe or something. I'm the one that should have had the lead in the play. I'm the one who should have been kissing Millicent. But when I tried to get her to kiss me she acted like I was creepy or something. I taught her a lesson. I showed her she couldn't treat me like dirt."

Katie's eyes stung and sweat dripped down her forehead, but she could not stop straining to free herself, even though she knew the effort was exhausting her.

"It's easy, now that I can drive," Rage went on placidly. "I can go wherever I want and I can put girls in my trunk and move them. I've done it three times now and nobody's got a clue it's me. I've got lots of pictures of them. This time, though, I'm going to do something bigger and better."

A muscle in his cheek twitched. His tongue flicked out to wet his lips, and Katie noticed that his grip on the rope was so tight his knuckles were white. For a second she allowed herself to hope he would make some mistake that would allow her to get away. But then, as if he read her thoughts, he said, "I'm not going to make any mistakes. This time Mr. P. is going to have a performance he'll never forget. Newspapers all over the country will cover it when my pipe bomb blows the whole place up. I'll be famous—sort of."

Looking amused, he rolled up the length of cord and stuffed it into the pocket of his leather pants. "I'd really like to choke you right now, but I've got to have something to remember you by, you know?" He smiled. "I'll be back. Don't go anywhere, huh?"

The metal door closed behind him, and Katie heard the click of the deadbolt sliding into place. She struggled to scream, but all she could manage were little whimpers deep in her throat. She slumped against the wall. It was hopeless. She might as well give up.

Chapter Twenty

Steve wondered how long he should wait before calling Katie's parents. He was sure something had gone wrong.

He opened the door to the big dressing room that was stage right. Guys were pulling their costumes over their heads. "What you waitin' for, Patton?" A chorister straightened his hat and checked himself in the mirror. "Get dressed, man."

"I think I'll go see if Katie's gotten here yet."

"Is this some new excuse to go by the girls' dressing room?"

Steve turned on his heel and left without answering. At the other side of the stage a girl in a slip scurried into the room just ahead of him. She squealed and closed the door in his face. He knocked on the door. "Hey, is Katie in there?" he yelled.

"She's not here yet!" called a voice from inside.

Mr. Panovitch bustled over to Steve, his jowls jiggling. "What's this about Katie? Is she late? And after I had emphasized in the *strongest* way possible that we were to be here on time—I must have said it a hundred times." He clutched at his belly. "An ulcer is brewing in my duodenum this very minute. If that prima donna imagines we'll hold the performance for her, she is *sadly* mistaken."

"I'm going to call her house," said Steve.

"You ought to be getting in costume, young man!" Mr. Panovitch called, but Steve ignored him.

A few members of the audience were already filing into their seats when Steve stepped into the auditorium. An alarm was ringing inside Steve's head like a siren. How could these people be standing around making small talk at a time like this? He dropped a quarter into the pay phone and dialed Katie's number. When her father answered, Steve quickly explained that Katie hadn't arrived yet.

"She left here almost an hour ago," said Mr. Sloan. "Are you sure she's not there?"

Steve hesitated. Maybe he had been too

quick to panic. He hadn't actually seen inside the girls' dressing room. "I didn't see her, and one of the girls told me she hadn't gotten here," he said awkwardly. "Maybe I'd better go check myself."

"Call me as soon as you find out something," said Mr. Sloan. Instead of going directly backstage, Steve pushed open the heavy doors to the auditorium and stepped outside. It was chillier now that the sun had gone down, but he scarcely noticed. He jogged toward the student parking lot. Maybe Katie was driving up right this minute, he thought, and he was getting all steamed about nothing. The bushes and trees beside the auditorium building kept him from having a clear view, so he ran over closer to the parking lot. He still couldn't see Katie's car.

He cast a glance in the direction of the sprawling complex of buildings that made up the school. He wondered if she had parked behind the school. But that didn't make sense. Why would she park farther away when there were still parking places left in the nearer student lot?

Steve trotted back to the auditorium. As soon as he reached the girls' dressing room, he threw the door open. Girls in slips clutched their costumes and made halfhearted efforts to conceal themselves behind clothing racks.

"Look, this is important." Steve's voice rang out harshly amid the titters. "Where is Katie? Has anybody seen her?"

The girls looked around in confusion. "Maybe she's already dressed," someone volunteered. "She usually is early, you know."

"What?" shrieked Mr. Panovitch, who had appeared at the dressing-room door. "Katie's still not here? Dear Lord, what else can go wrong? A plague of locusts is no doubt waiting in the wings." His nostrils were white and pinched. "What are you doing in the girls' dressing room, Steve? And where is Katie? This is beyond everything. Nicole, you may have to go on in Katie's place."

Nicole shook her head.

"Don't be stupid," snapped Mr. Panovitch. "I know you've been helping her learn her lines. You probably know them better than she does. We'll cut the leprechaun's solo dance. Just be sure to step forward when it's time for Steve to kiss you."

"But where is Katie?" Steve repeated.

"I can't worry about her now," said Mr. Panovitch. "I've got too much to think about. The show must go on!"

Mr. Panovitch looked really upset as he hurried away. It struck Steve that Mr. Panovitch actually thought the play was important.

"Get dressed!" Mr. Panovitch shouted at Steve. "Why aren't you dressed? I must have co-operation!"

"Something's happened to Katie," Steve snapped. "She could be hurt—or dead. The last thing I'm worried about is the show."

"I won't be spoken to in that manner!" screamed Mr. Panovitch. "Defy me, will you? Mark my words, you'll never act in this school again!"

"Katie's here." Nicole spoke suddenly. Her face was as white as her blouse.

Steve strode over to her through a crowd of half-clothed girls and grabbed her by the shoulders. "What do you mean? She's here? Have you seen her?"

He could feel Nicole quivering. "No," she whispered, "but she's here. I can feel her presence."

"Is this one of your psychic bits?" He turned away from her. "Great timing, Nicole. Just what we need right now, a little theater. Give me a break." Disgusted, he stormed out of the room.

When he reached the lobby, he called the Sloans again. "She's not here," he reported to Katie's father. "I checked the parking lot and the dressing room. Nobody's seen her."

"I'm on my way," Mr. Sloan said. "Katie's mother is going to call the police. I'm going to try to retrace her path. If you hear anything, Steve, anything at all, call here. Katie's mother is going to stand by in case there's any word."

"Yes, sir." The fear in Mr. Sloan's voice was like fuel for Steve's own raging panic. Where could Katie be? How could she vanish between her house and the school? Maybe he should set out toward her house and meet Mr. Sloan halfway. There was a lot of ground to search between the house and the school, and it would be easier with two of them working on it.

Steve could not allow himself to think of what might have happened to Katie. He only focused on one thought—he had to find her. Soon.

Chapter Twenty-one

Katie's hands and ankles were tied so tightly that it was almost impossible for her to move, but she knew she had to. If she could even get in a position where she could knock something down and make some noise, she might have a chance. Straining every muscle, she managed to wiggle so that she moved sideways on the gritty floor. Each inch seemed to take an eternity and she ached with the effort, but at last she was clear of the sink. Her head bumped against the wall. Sweat dripped in her eyes and blurred her vision. If only she could push herself up, she thought, and somehow stand. But then what? The door was locked. And even if she succeeded in thumping around the room, no one would hear her. No one came by the alley behind the auditorium. The sharp ticking sound in her brain, insistent and monotonous, seemed to say time was running out.

The bomb! She suddenly remembered that Rage had mentioned a bomb. She managed to struggle up to a half sitting position against the wall, her stomach muscles hurting from the effort. Looking around the room, she saw only a worn suitcase and a folded blanket arranged on the cot. The ticking sounded louder now that she had realized it might be the bomb. For a moment she froze, immobilized by her terror. She wondered if she might somehow set the thing off by thrashing about. But if she didn't free herself, Rage would kill her. He had only gone to get his camera to take a picture before strangling her.

Possibly by now, on the other side of the wall, there were people who could save her. Katie wasn't sure about the layout of the building and where the janitor's little room fit into the plan of things, but she knew that in a building crowded with people, the chances were that someone was close by. Maybe she could somehow make them hear her.

Nicole bent over to buckle her green slippers. Suddenly a thump startled her. She looked around, but only the blank wall was behind her.

She tried to thread the leather strap through the buckle, but her fingers were shaking too much.

Mr. Panovitch stuck his head in the dressing-room door. "Hurry, Nicole!" he cried shrilly. "You're on in the next scene."

"I—I can't." Nicole stared at him. She felt rooted to her chair.

"You most certainly can!" The drama coach stamped his foot. "I've had enough of you people. If you aren't standing in the wings in two minutes flat I will carry you on stage myself!" He slammed the door to the dressing room.

Nicole looked down at her trembling fingers. How could she go on? Something was dreadfully wrong. She could feel Katie's terror.

The smooth clicking sound of metal against metal drew Katie's fascinated eyes toward the door. A key was opening the lock. Rage was coming back!

The door opened and she was startled to see the pale, astonished face of the janitor.

"What're you doing in my room?" he gasped. He steadied himself with one hand against the doorjamb.

Katie struggled to cry out, trying to warn him, but only a muffled whimper escaped her. She watched helplessly as a dark shape loomed behind the janitor. Katie heard a sickening thud and saw the janitor's body jolted by a blow from behind. His face went blank with shock. Then his head drooped suddenly and he fell to his knees. He toppled over, falling face first against Katie in the small room. Katie gazed at his prone body in astonishment. Could a person die so quickly? But then to her relief she noticed a faintly perceptible movement of his shirt. He was still breathing.

The floor of the little room was so crowded that Rage would have to step on top of the janitor's body to get to her now. Standing in the doorway, Rage seemed to fill up what was left of the space in the room. He had put a leather bomber jacket over his sweater and he seemed larger than he had before. He knelt to pick up a manila envelope that lay at his feet. Propping it on a corner of the sink, he closed the door behind him. Then he took the length of cord out of his pocket. At the sight of it, Katie went rigid. But instead of coming at her, as she expected, he pulled the janitor's limp arms behind his back and tied them together. Katie watched him run the strong cord around and between the man's wrists three times and understood why she had been unable to free herself.

Rage finished tying the knot with a confident snap of the cord and stepped back. "The guy must've had a bad heart or something," he muttered. "He's not dead yet, but he will be soon enough—when the bomb goes off. This is the biggest one I've ever made. I blew off some little ones in the woods out by the reservoir to make sure I had it right. Ka-boom!" He grinned. "Amazing what you can do in your basement with some pipes and gelignite. When the play starts, it's arrivederci, baby. You'll be blown to smithereens." Rage chuckled. "What a fantastic opening night. Hear that ticking? That's the bomb."

Katie's eyes were drawn to the suitcase on the bed. She realized suddenly that the bomb must be inside it.

A sudden flash blinded her, and for a horrible moment she thought the bomb had gone off. But she was still alive. When she glanced at Rage, he was holding a camera. "You're very pretty," he cooed softly. "I could kill you now. Slowly." He took a step toward her and when Katie's eyes opened wide in fear, the flash went off in her eyes. "You're really scared, aren't you?" He sounded pleased. He stood framed by the dirty beige doorway, a weasly-looking boy with a weak chin and a small mouth. Katie was astonished that she had never noticed his cruelty. She had always thought that surly manner was a front, that he was only trying to seem cool.

Underneath, she had assumed, he was the same as everyone else.

"I brought you something," he said. He pulled a sheaf of shiny eight-by-ten photographs from the manila envelope. "Look at this." He brandished one at Katie. Her stomach heaved when she recognized Millicent's face, her mouth slack and her eyes dull. Katie didn't have to ask herself what the subjects were of the other pictures—they were his other victims. And he planned to add her face to his gallery! She struggled vainly against her bonds as Rage clutched the sheaf of pictures awkwardly to his chest.

"Look at me!" he boasted. "People would never guess that I'm so important. Of course, I could get in big trouble if people knew. That's why I keep it secret. It's better if they think the strangler is somebody else." He frowned down at the janitor. "I think I may pin this one on him. Everybody suspects him anyway. I hadn't thought of it before, but now I see it's perfect. This is the janitor's room, so it all fits. I stole his key and got a copy made. He thought he just lost it—idiot. I don't want to kill him right now, because they could tell he was dead before the bomb went off when they do the autopsy. It ought to look like he just came in here to check on the bomb and sort of miscalculated." He glanced at his watch. "Which reminds me—I must be careful not to do that."

He stuffed the photos back into the large envelope. "Too bad nobody appreciates me. But you know I'm a genius, don't you, Katie?" He stepped outside and Katie again heard the click of the deadbolt slipping into place.

Steve was about to get in his car when he stopped abruptly. What if there was some sense in what Nicole had said? What if Katie was here at school? He didn't really believe Nicole was psychic, but when she had said "Katie's here" it had made his flesh creep.

Besides, in a way, it made sense. Both of the murderer's victims had gone to this school. Wasn't it possible the school was connected to the murders? It wouldn't be a bad idea to start by searching here. He remembered that when something was mislaid, his grandmother used to say "Look where it's supposed to be. And then look again." He could start with the auditorium.

Steve headed back toward the building. He'd gotten as far as the bushes beside the building when Rage appeared.

"What are you doing out here?" Steve cried, startled. Rage had come up from nowhere, as if he'd stepped out from behind one of the bushes. "I thought you'd be on stage by now," Steve added.

Rage shrugged. "Decided to give it a miss. I'm only in the chorus. They won't even know I'm not there."

"You heard about Katie being missing, didn't you?" Steve asked. A wave of gratitude swept over him. Maybe in the past he'd thought Rage had gotten pretty strange, but he noticed that nobody else was volunteering to help him look. All the rest of them were going on with the play as if nothing had happened. Only Rage was willing to stand up to Mr. Panovitch. "Nicole thinks Katie's around here somewhere." Steve frowned. "I don't know—I'm starting to wonder if she's right. We've got to search every inch of this school—I mean knock on every door, look under every stairway. I never thought I'd say this, but something tells me Nicole may actually be right about Katie being here at school."

"We'd better split up the school grounds," Rage said promptly. "I'll start on this side with the auditorium building, and you can go around to the gym and start there."

"Right," said Steve. He loped away across the front of the auditorium and back toward the gym, his heart beating with a dreadful urgency. *Hurry, hurry,* a voice inside him said. In the back of his mind, he knew that Katie might already be dead, but in his heart he couldn't believe it. He felt he was in a race against the murderer and that he would find her somehow.

Steve glanced around the parking area behind the gym. The huge gymnasium loomed over him, its high windows glittering blankly, reflecting the light of the street lamp.

Steve tried the front door. "Katie?" he yelled. "Katie? Are you in there?" He knew it was useless to yell, since she might be unconscious. She could be right on the other side of the door and he wouldn't have any way of knowing it. The janitor would have a passkey to the buildings, but Steve didn't know where to find him since he had quit. He might even be the one who had taken Katie. Steve wondered frantically if his stepfather could pull some strings and get a key from the principal. But there was no time for that. He ran around to the side door and began banging on it hard. Suddenly he stopped.

Something was wrong. Why was he at the gym when Rage was at the auditorium? Steve frowned, his eyes scanning the dark buildings restlessly. What made him feel something odd was going on with Rage? Only moments before he had been grateful for Rage's offer to help. Now he wasn't so sure. Why?

A second later he realized what was bothering him. Rage had taken the lead, that was what seemed so wrong. "You go to the gym and I'll take the auditorium," he had said, as if he were in charge. It wasn't like him. He was more the whiny, follower type. Passive—that was the word for him. It was completely out of character for him to direct the search. And why would he be so concerned about Katie, anyway? Unless, like Nicole, Rage knew something the others didn't know.

"Next I'll be thinking we're all psychic like stupid Nicole," Steve thought. But his nagging suspicion would not go away. The way Rage acted made no sense unless . . .

Steve suddenly wheeled around and began running back toward the auditorium.

Chapter Twenty-two

Steve ran fast, cutting across the campus, dodging around the classroom buildings. Gasping for air, he saw the back corner of the auditorium directly ahead of him as he came up around the industrial arts building. He glanced into the darkness of the narrow corridor between the buildings. The alley was as good a place to start looking as any. In fact, because it was so obscure and dark, it was precisely the place the murderer might be hiding.

"Katie?" he called. His voice, confined by the two buildings, echoed faintly. Cautiously, he moved down the corridor, half expecting someone to jump out at him from behind the staircase ahead. "Katie?" His own voice sounded strange in the tight space between the buildings.

When he came up to the staircase, his foot hit something soft and he looked down. It was a shoe! He bent to pick it up. When he turned it over he saw it was a simple black ballerina slipper. He wished he had paid more attention to Katie's clothes. Fingering it, he decided that it couldn't have been outside for long, because it felt reasonably stiff and had a shape. His heart quickened. Maybe it was Katie's, after all. He tucked it under his belt. "Katie!" he bellowed. "Katie!"

And then he heard it. A thump. He jerked toward the sound and suddenly saw the door in the smoothness of the corridor's other wall. The metal had been painted to match the wall, and the door was flush and tight. When he stood directly in front of it, he was alarmed to see there was a smear of something dark on the doorjamb. Blood? His heart seemed to be throbbing painfully in his throat as he tried the door. "Katie!" he yelled. "Are you in there?" There was another thump. Then a shaky male voice said, "We're locked in. We're tied up."

Steve was so startled he backed away from the door. What was going on? "Katie, are you in there?" he repeated urgently. "What's going on?"

"Steve," Katie sounded breathless. "We just

got my gag off. We're tied up and we can't get the knots out. It's hopeless."

Steve backed away and took a running jump at the door. He bounced off the metal, grabbed his shoulder, and winced. It was a solid steel door, he judged, and wasn't about to give way. "Who's got the key?" he called. "I could go get help, but I don't want to leave you here in case he comes back."

He could hear her coughing. "Are you all right, Katie?" he asked anxiously. "Can't you unlock it from inside?"

"It's a deadbolt. It's no use. And Steve—there's a bomb in here! Rage wants to blow up the whole building." Katie spoke in a choked voice. "Steve, try to get a passkey."

"There isn't any passkey," moaned the janitor. "I put the deadbolt on the door myself so nobody would mess with my stuff."

"We can cut into the door with an acetylene torch," Steve said, hoping he sounded confident.

"There isn't time. The bomb could go off any minute! Rage said it's supposed to go off during the play, and I can hear it ticking."

"Wait a minute!" Steve said. "If the janitor put the lock on the door, he must have the key. Maybe it's on him somewhere."

"I d-dropped it," quavered the janitor.

"Where?" Katie cried. "You must have unlocked the door with it tonight. You would have had to use it to get in."

"I don't know. When that boy jumped me I must have dropped it. I figured I'd better play dead then or he'd kill me, so I pretended to pass out. He was trying to pin the murders on me! I knew somebody was trying to frame me." The janitor's voice began to rise hysterically.

Steve fell to his knees and felt frantically around the door. The surface of the concrete was rough against his fingertips, but he felt nothing that could be a key. Then, as his fingertips brushed against the ground where the walkway met the wall, he heard a faint metallic clink. The key must have been propped up against the doorjamb. "I've got it!" he yelled. A second later, he was turning it in the lock.

Steve flung the door open. His heart twisted inside him when he saw that the corners of Katie's mouth were puffy and red from the gag that now lay limp around her neck. "Untie us!" she cried. "We've got to get out of here."

"Don't worry," Steve said. A shiver ran through him as he quickly untied Katie's wrists and ankles. He remembered that he and Rage had practiced tying these same complicated sailor's knots when they were kids. Why hadn't he realized then all the darkness that was inside Rage?

"Don't forget me!" the janitor whispered anxiously. "I'm tied up, too."

As Steve struggled with the second set of knots, his eye was drawn to the ticking suitcase on the cot. As soon as he had freed the janitor, Steve jumped for the suitcase.

"Don't touch it!" Katie screeched. "You'll make it go off!"

Steve drew his hand back. He remembered reading in the newspaper about bomb-squad people being blown up when they tried to disarm a bomb. Katie was right, it was too risky to try to throw it outside the room. Better not to touch it. "Okay," he said, "but move, Katie! Let's get out of here."

But when Katie tried to run, she stumbled and fell against the door. The red welts around her ankles made anger surge inside Steve. It would have been a pleasure for him to hold Rage down and give him a dose of his own medicine. Hurriedly, Steve swept Katie up in his arms and carried her out. "Come on," he said over his shoulder. "Follow me." But the janitor stood motionless and dazed under the bare light bulb. "Move!" Steve urged him. "Run! It could blow up anytime."

The janitor began limping after them.

"We've got to warn the others," Steve said, putting Katie down on the sidewalk. "We've got to get everybody out of the auditorium."

Katie limped along beside Steve, the janitor following with tottering steps. Impatience swelled inside Steve until he could have screamed. Penned in by the tall buildings on either side, he felt trapped and desperate. He knew the alley was the worst place to be if the bomb went off—the explosion would be contained by the buildings on either side. "Come on!" he urged desperately. "Hurry!"

Overhead Steve could make out the faintly luminous sky. What would he have done if he had not been able to find the key? He shuddered.

Steve breathed easier when they were out of the corridor and in the open. Ahead of them was the student parking lot filled with lines of cars, their hoods gleaming under the parking lot lights. To the left lay the patch of trees and bushes that flanked the auditorium. In the opposite direction lay the vast playing fields and the woods beyond them. Rage could be anywhere. It wasn't safe to leave Katie and the janitor alone, yet Steve knew he should be running around to the front of the auditorium to warn the others. He stood still a moment, painfully torn by indecision. Then he scooped Katie up in his arms.

"We've got to run out front and warn the others," he told the janitor. "Go out by the road. You ought to be okay out there. There'll be cars going by."

"Put me down!" Katie cried. "What if you fall, running with me like this? This is crazy."

Steve put her down but held her hand in a tight grip and pulled her along with him as he ran toward the front of the building. "I'm not letting you out of my sight," he panted. "No matter what."

Dragging Katie with him, he pressed through the tangle of bushes and out to the front of the auditorium. When they were standing in front of the big glass doors, he released her hand. It made no sense to take her inside the auditorium when the whole place might blow up any second. "Okay," he said. "You go out by the road, too. Flag down some cars or something."

"What are you going to do?" she cried.

"I'm going to try to warn the others."

When Steve opened the door, strains of music incongruously wafted into the night. The band was playing and the entire chorus was singing about a pot of gold at the end of the rainbow. He glanced briefly over his shoulder to assure himself that Katie was going out to the road, then he ran into the auditorium.

He attracted some curious stares as he sped

down the center aisle. Halfway to the stage he stopped and turned around. The band was playing and the chorus danced onstage. He raised his voice to be heard over them. "I have an announcement!" he said. "There's been a bomb threat. You need to file out of the auditorium as fast as possible."

Some of the people nearest him pointed at him and murmured to each other, but to his amazement, no one made any attempt to stand up. Their inertia infuriated him. He felt powerless, as if he were in an awful dream where he was unable to move.

"Steve!" Turning his head, Steve recognized Mike Green's mother. "What's wrong?" she asked.

"There's a bomb in the back of the building," he explained. "We need to get out of here."

Mrs. Green, a plump, middle-aged woman, stood up and motioned to the others in her row to follow. The murmur of sound grew to a buzz. Steve could hear feet shuffling on the cement floor as people began moving toward the exit.

Incredibly, the band was still playing, though the elves dancing up on the stage were darting uneasy glances at their exiting audience. Steve strode into the midst of the orchestra. "What's going on?" asked Mr. Bates, the band director.

"A bomb," said Steve. "You need to get the band out of here."

Mr. Bates cut the band off and barked, "Clarinets, first. An orderly exit to the left and right, please." Folding chairs and music stands toppled as the band, clutching instruments, began stumbling toward the red exit lights.

Steve made his way through the middle of the orchestra pit and shouted up at the stage. "Break it up! There's a bomb in the building."

"Where are the cops, Steve?" Mike Green yelled down at him. A few members of the chorus leapfrogged over the footlights and others followed their example. Cast members began streaming down the side stairs of the stage and lined up close on the heels of the band.

"What happened to Katie?" Nicole stared down at Steve over the footlights, her face pale under her green leprechaun cap.

"She's okay!" said Steve. "Get out of here! Tell the others. Rage put a bomb in the back of the building."

The kids at the side exits, picking up on the panic in Steve's voice, began bunching and falling over each other.

"Don't run," Mr. Bates screeched. "Trumpets! You heard me!"

Mr. Panovitch appeared on the stage, his face pink with emotion. "I won't have this,

Steve. It's not funny. I'll see that you're expelled for this!"

"The auditorium could go up in flames any minute," yelled Steve, "and if anybody's backstage they're practically sitting on the bomb. It's going to be your fault if it blows up on them."

"Oooo, this is beyond everything!" Mr. Panovitch stamped his foot. But to Steve's relief, he disappeared backstage. A moment or two later, some confused-looking kids came out the side doors to the stage followed by a puffing Mr. Panovitch.

"Better not to take chances," Mr. Bates boomed as he ushered the stragglers from the band out the side doors. "Stand well away from the building."

Nicole tumbled into the orchestra pit and joined the general exodus.

"Get everybody out front," Steve yelled. "Out by the street." His nerves were raw, and every second he expected to see the walls tumble and the cavernous room collapse.

"Out front," he shouted as soon as he stepped out into the cool night air. "Get everybody away from the building."

When he rounded the thick patch of bushes, he was relieved to see the blinking blue light of a police car. He ran toward it and found Katie and the janitor. A police officer with a bullhorn stood in front of the big glass doors. "Stand away from the building!" he boomed. "Stand back."

"The bomb squad is on the way," the police officer in the car explained. "Our problem now is making sure everybody is out."

"Can you call Katie's house?" Steve asked. "Her dad is out looking for her, and he must be worried sick."

"I'll call headquarters," said the officer. "What's their number?"

Mr. Panovitch puffed up to the police car. "Mr. P., is everybody out?" Katie asked.

"How should I know?" Mr. Panovitch screamed. "Nobody tells me anything. I refuse to take any responsibility!"

The officer with the bullhorn shrugged, pushed open the glass doors, and went in. Steve could hear the muffled sounds of the bullhorn from within the building.

Chapter Twenty-three

An old dirt road, rutted and choked with weeds, ran through the woods that lay behind the playing fields of the school. Rage's blue Plymouth was parked there, right in front of Katie's car. The door of the Plymouth was flung open so that the inside light was on. There was little chance of anyone's seeing the light, because the woods were thick between the car and the playing fields. Rage switched on the tape player—the excited riff of the drums suited his mood—but he kept it turned low. No sense taking chances.

He pulled the sheaf of glossies out of their manila envelope and gloated. The best was yet to come. He would develop the picture of Katie himself. It wasn't the kind of thing a person could send to Quick Print. The snapshot of Steve's stepmother lay on top. Her swollen face was bleached by the flash. He had been rattled when he took that and had gotten too close. The one of Laurie was better. It was particularly well lit, since he had taken it in the clear early-morning light. But up till now none of the shots showed what he most wanted—the fear in their eyes. That was why the picture he took of Katie would be the best one. He only hoped he had not done something stupid like load the film wrong. But he knew he was too smart to mess up. Hadn't he committed three murders and gotten away with it? He shuffled through the pictures again, smiling.

Something was wrong, he realized suddenly, his smile fading. Millicent wasn't there. He threw himself down on the front seat and frantically felt under the seat. Millicent's picture had to be here. Perhaps it had slipped over the other side of the seat. He scrambled out of the car and ran around to the other side. But when he opened the door he saw nothing but a crumpled Flakey's bag. His spine went stiff with anxiety. Maybe it had slipped out of his grasp when he was showing it to Katie. It had been so crowded in that little room, so awkward to maneuver. He clutched at his envelope and shuffled through the pictures, turning each one over, his hands clammy with fear. It had to be here! It must be stuck to another picture, or he had overlooked it somehow. But no, it was gone.

How often had he sat in his room poring over his precious photographs, thumbing lovingly through them? His fingerprints must be all over each glossy surface. What if the photo somehow happened to survive the bomb? It could be the evidence that sent him to the electric chair!

He had broken into a stumbling run almost before he had made any conscious decision to return to the little room. The car, its door open and its inside light on, sat humming with music on the dirt road as Rage ran headlong through the woods, stumbling over undergrowth in blind panic. He could do it—he could still make things right—he only needed to fix this one small thing. He bolted across the football field, his boots sinking into the soft ground.

In front of the building, a fire truck screeched to a halt behind the police car. Two more trucks were right behind it. Fire fighters leaped off the trucks and snaked hoses in the direction of the fire hydrant.

"Stand clear," the police bullhorn trumpeted. The crowd shrank away from the building. Katie glanced over her shoulder at the police car. Its radio crackled with some garbled message she couldn't decipher.

"I saw an explosion once in St. Paul, Minnesota," the janitor told Katie confidentially. "It was a building demolition. They did it on purpose. Not like this." Whether it was the dim light or Katie's own heightened consciousness of the craziness of life, the janitor seemed, at the moment, almost normal.

How could she not have known that Rage was the strangler? She felt stupid, as if what had happened were somehow her fault. Surely there had been some sign that he was not to be trusted. If so, she had not been clever enough to see it. She had walked right into his trap. And he had fooled Millicent and Laurie, too. Katie blinked away tears. She knew she had been lucky to escape. If Steve had not come looking for her . . . Whenever she thought about how she had suspected him she felt terrible. Glad he could not read her mind, she glanced over at him.

"I wish I knew where Rage was," Steve said. He had propped a foot on the bumper of the police car and was doing his best to seem calm.

She knew that he could not have suspected Rage either until the very last. Though he had made the connection between his stepmother's murder and the similar murders of Millicent and Laurie, still he had not thought of Rage. How could they have ever suspected that it was Rage? Rage, who ate in the cafeteria and did algebra homework like the rest of them.

"Don't worry, son," said a policeman. "We're putting out an APB on the car, and a car's on the way over to his house right now. We'll get him."

"You heard what he said," Katie told Steve. "Everything's going to be all right. They're going to catch him."

"They'd better," said Steve grimly. "We need a confession."

Katie realized Steve was worried about proving his father's innocence. "He told me he killed your stepmother," she said.

Steve's foot slipped off the fender, and he stared at her. "You're kidding me! He did?"

"While I was tied up he stood there bragging about how he'd taken you down a peg by pinning the murder on your dad."

Steve's hands tightened into fists, and for a minute he didn't speak. Then he said bleakly, "I bet it's pretty hard to get somebody out of prison when they've already been convicted."

"You mean you think the police won't believe me?"

"It's not like you're an impartial witness, is it? I just hope Rage doesn't kill himself or something like that. We need his confession!"

A couple of fire fighters pushed past them

wearing heavy black rubber coats and carrying big flashlights.

Nicole ran over to Katie and hugged her. "Katie, you're okay!" Tears streaked down her cheeks. "You're okay!"

"I'm fine," Katie said weakly. But she felt as if she could burst into tears herself any minute.

Rasping breaths tore Rage's throat as he ran. When he reached the door to the room, he had to force himself to keep his hands steady to fit the key into the lock. Dimly he was aware of some booming sound and background noise, but he concentrated everything, every muscle, on turning the key.

Everything is perfect, he thought, except for losing the photo. I can get it back. I can make everything right again. His twist of the key should have unlocked the door, but it hadn't. Vaguely puzzled, he turned it in the other direction. This time, when he heard it click, he was able to open the door. The light was still on, but the room was empty. He stared, bewildered. Where could they be? He saw his precious photograph lying facedown on the floor, a black heel mark on its middle. Sobbing, he fell to his knees and snatched it up. Suddenly a blast lifted him off his feet and he felt a shattering instant of blinding pain.

* * *

The crowd at the front of the school heard the explosion. Katie watched in amazement as the ground trembled and a cloud of powder rose from the back of the building. The big glass doors dissolved into shards, spraying some of the nearby crowd with slivers of glass. There were screams as the fire fighters arched streams of water toward the blaze.

"Stand back!" a voice boomed through the bullhorn. "Stand away."

The crowd stood silent, staring at the burning building. Except for the broken glass, the front of the building looked untouched, but at the back it had crumbled.

A fragment of foam insulation settled at Katie's feet, blown by the blast. Glancing down at it uneasily, she edged farther away.

The Sloans' station wagon pulled up beyond the fire trucks. Her parents got out and ran to her.

"Thank God," Mrs. Sloan sobbed, holding Katie tight. "My baby! You're all right."

The smell of her mother's perfume was amazingly comforting. When her father threw his arms around them both, Katie snuggled close, feeling her parents' warmth. Warm and safe, she thought. At last.

Chapter Twenty-Four

School was canceled on Monday. The police were still poking around in the rubble of the auditorium. The entire area smelled strongly of smoke and had been roped off by yellow tape that said "Crime Scene—Do Not Cross."

Nicole called Katie's house Monday afternoon to report that the police had found Rage's body in the ruins of the auditorium building.

"Are they absolutely sure that the body they found was his?" asked Katie nervously. "I keep expecting him to jump out at me from behind some dark corner."

"Absolutely sure," Nicole said. "The police told Dad that they matched up the teeth with Rage's dental records."

Katie clutched at her stomach. So the body

had been unrecognizable. She could have ended up that way if Steve had not come looking for her.

It was comforting to know that Rage was dead, truly dead, and that he could not hurt her anymore.

She spent most of that afternoon at the police station swearing out an affidavit attesting that Rage had confessed to her that he had murdered Mrs. Schulemburger.

The police had already found Rage's car parked by Katie's in the woods. In the Plymouth was a manila envelope of pictures, including a photo of Steve's stepmother. The police at the station told Katie that under the circumstances there would be no difficulty getting the governor to order Steve's father released at once.

As soon as Katie got home, she called Steve and told him the news. "The police called here already," he said. "They need somebody to identify the picture they found of Judy. I'm going to Tyler Falls in a few days." She could hear the happiness in his voice. "I talked to an old friend of my dad's and he says some of my dad's buddies at the bank are going to have a big party for him as soon as he gets out."

"Don't you love happy endings?" Katie asked. "You'll be here for the cast party, though, won't you?"

"What cast party? They didn't even finish the play, Katie. What's to celebrate?"

"All I know is Nicole is sending a petition around and she says she's going to take it to Mr. P. personally. After all, it's not our fault that the play was—" She hesitated.

"A bomb?" Steve laughed. "Okay, I promise I'll try my best to make it to the party."

"You won't be sorry. Our cast parties are famous," Katie assured him.

Friday night found the cafeteria transformed for the cast's festivities. The cafeteria tables had been stacked in the corners, and now crepe paper streamers dangled from the light fixtures. Chorus members dressed as leprechauns milled around, half dazed by the noise level.

"This is the best cast party yet," Mike Green yelled, raising his voice to be heard over the din. "I never thought we'd get Mr. P. to agree to it."

"It wasn't our fault the auditorium blew up," Nicole said.

"So, your eloquent petition changed his mind?" Mike asked.

Bryan shook his head. "Nope. I think what did the trick was Nicole telling him she'd had a vision that unless we had a cast party, his next production would have a curse on it."

"You didn't, Nic!" Katie said.

"I believe I have some credibility these days as a psychic," Nicole said. She held out a bowl of potato chips to Tracy, who gingerly took a handful of them. Her head immobilized by a metal halo, Tracy sat stiffly in one of the few chairs.

Nicole regarded her quizzically. "Can you bathe in that thing? How does it work, anyway?"

"It's very simple," said Tracy gloomily. "They screw it into your skull in front and your hipbones on the side and you can't turn your head for six weeks."

"Only five weeks to go," Mike told her cheerfully.

"I may scream," said Tracy.

"At least they caught the guy that did it," said Nicole.

"They did?" Steve asked. "Hey, I didn't know that."

"You've had your mind on other things," Katie said gently.

"It was a thirteen-year-old kid that hit me, can you believe it?" said Tracy. "I wish he was the one in this brace. That would teach him to drive without a license. It's so unfair that he's the one who broke the law and I'm the one who ended up stuck in the brace."

"You're lucky to be alive." Nicole grabbed a handful of potato chips.

"Thank you," said Tracy icily. "That's just what I'm feeling right now—lucky."

"I was so sure it was the janitor who had run you down," Katie said. "Boy, did I have it all wrong. I never suspected Rage of being the murderer. I *trusted* him. When I got to the school and saw that he was already there, I was actually glad to see him. What an idiot I was!"

"That'll teach you to get there early," said Nicole. "He knew you would, just like he knew Laurie went jogging every morning."

"I said all along it had to be somebody we knew," Tracy said.

"Katie's lucky to be alive," said Nicole.

"Cut it out, Nic," Katie said. "None of us wants to hear how lucky we are. Got it?"

"All right! All right!"

"For that matter, if Steve hadn't tracked me down all of us would have gotten blown up in the biggest grand finale number in school history. Steve's a hero." Katie beamed at him.

"You can sing 'For He's a Jolly Good Fellow,'" said Steve. "But let's skip the cake and dancing girls. I'm a modest man."

Nicole frowned at Tracy. "Not that we aren't glad to see you, Tracy, but you weren't exactly in the play, were you?"

"She's here as my date." Mike Green put his hand on Tracy's back and smiled at her. "I've always been drawn to glamor."

"Mr. P. told me he's already thinking about his next production," Nicole said. "Maybe you should try out for it, Tracy."

"Well, he can count me out," Steve said. "Can you imagine—Katie was about to be murdered any minute and he kept saying 'the show must go on.'"

"I know he's kind of strange, but isn't anybody even curious about what the next play is going to be?" Nicole asked.

"We're just dying to know," Bryan said.

"Well, get this—he said that this time he wanted to do something closer to our experience. No leprechauns. Something more like real life."

"*Our Town*," guessed Mike.

"*Dracula*," said Nicole with heavy emphasis.

Katie choked with laughter.

Here's a preview of Room 13,
the second book in the Nightmare Inn *series,*
also from HarperPaperbacks.

The Naughtons arrived at the New Arcadia Inn late on a foggy Friday night. They'd been driving down a dark road through a forest when the large white colonial inn seemed to appear out of nowhere. Mr. Naughton had booked a two-bedroom suite. Erin had to share the second bedroom with Bobby.

At breakfast early the next morning, Erin sulked in her chair and stared through her sunglasses at the other guests of the inn. There weren't many people in the dining room at that hour, and those who were there looked old.

Not only had her father made her miss the Last Dance, but now she had to spend the next four days with a bunch of geriatric cases.

Erin's parents and brother came back from

the buffet. Her mother's and brother's plates were filled with pancakes, sausage, and eggs. Mr. Naughton had a single bowl of oat-bran cereal, some fresh strawberries, and a glass of orange juice.

"Aren't you going to get some breakfast?" her mother asked Erin as they sat down around the circular table covered with a white tablecloth.

Erin shook her head.

"You have to eat something," Mrs. Naughton said.

"I'll have bread and water," Erin said sullenly as she reached for the bread basket.

"This isn't prison," Bobby said.

"It *feels* like it is," Erin snapped, glaring at her father.

Mr. Naughton's face darkened. "We know you're unhappy about not going to the dance, Erin. We've been over it a thousand times. Now we're here, and I think it's about time you got over it."

Erin frowned.

"Erin, darling, please take off those sunglasses while we're eating," her mother said.

Erin slowly took off the glasses and put them on the table beside her.

"Hey, be philosophical," Bobby said. He was already halfway through a tall stack of pancakes drenched in maple syrup. "The dance was last night. It's over now, so you might as well enjoy yourself."

"Maybe your brother's right, honey," Mrs. Naughton said.

Erin shrugged. A girl around her age, wearing black pants and a white blouse, pushed a cart toward their table. She had curly, bright-red hair and a gold name tag that identified her as Sarah. As she cleared some of the plates and refilled the water glasses, she stared at Erin. Erin felt a strange chill and looked away.

"How can I enjoy myself?" Erin asked. "Look around. Everyone here is ancient. This place probably doubles as an old-age home."

No sooner were the words out of her mouth than a boy and a girl about her age entered the dining room. They were both tall and slender. The girl had long black hair pulled back into a thick ponytail. The boy's hair was blond and curly. Each of them had on a white T-shirt over a bathing suit.

"There are some young people," Mr. Naughton said. "Why don't you go over and introduce yourself?"

"Oh, sure," Erin said sourly. "I'll just go over and say, 'Hi, I'm Erin Naughton and I want to hang out with you.'"

"It looks like they're going swimming," Mrs.

Naughton said. "Maybe you could go down to the pool."

Erin looked at her mother and father with surprise. "You mean I'm not scheduled to spend every waking minute doing something with the family?"

Her father frowned. "I'm getting tired of your lip, young lady."

Mrs. Naughton put a hand on her husband's shoulder. "Now, Henry, remember what the doctor said. You have to try to avoid stressful situations."

"You could have avoided a lot of stress if you'd let me stay at Kira's this weekend," Erin said.

"I said that's enough," Mr. Naughton said, glowering.

"Your father's right, Erin," Mrs. Naughton said. "Give it a rest, will you? Now, your father and I are playing golf this morning. You and Bobby are free to do whatever you want until lunchtime, when we'll meet you back here."

"I know what I'm doing," Bobby said. "You know that video room we passed in the hall? It's got the Terminator game."

"Try not to waste all your money on it," Erin's father said.

"No way," Bobby said. "I've played that game

a million times. I can make a couple bucks last all morning."

"And what do you think you'll do, Erin?" Mrs. Naughton asked.

Erin shrugged. She was tempted to make a wisecrack, but she knew it would just make her parents angry. Besides, she had a few hours of freedom. That was better than none at all.

"Maybe I'll just take a walk," she said.

As Erin left the dining room after breakfast, she realized that she'd left behind her sunglasses. Walking back toward the table, she saw Sarah, the waitress with the bright-red hair, clearing the dirty dishes. Erin looked around, but her glasses weren't there.

"Uh, excuse me," she said. "I think I left a pair of sunglasses here. Did you see them?"

Sarah looked up and stared at her for a moment. Then she shook her head.

"Are you sure?" Erin asked. "I mean, we were just sitting here. I know I left them."

"I never saw them," Sarah said in a flat voice, and continued clearing the plates.

Erin frowned. She bent down and looked under the table, but her sunglasses weren't on the floor. Could Sarah have taken them? The only other possibility was that someone had walked by and taken them just after she and her family got up. Erin looked around and decided that was impossible. There simply hadn't been enough time for anyone to do that.

"You're absolutely sure you didn't see them?" she asked Sarah again.

The red-haired girl shook her head slowly. Erin didn't know what to think. Was she lying?

"Well, let me give you my room number," Erin said. "If anyone finds them they can leave them at the front desk."

Sarah nodded and turned away to continue clearing the table.

"Wait, I haven't told you my room number," Erin said. "It's—"

"Two eighteen," Sarah said.

Erin stared at her. "How'd you know that?"

Sarah blinked. "I saw you come out of it this morning."

"Oh." Erin turned to go, but she was puzzled. She didn't remember seeing anyone in the hall when she had left her room that morning.

Back in her room, Erin turned on the TV. The only programs on were boring news shows and cartoons. Fortunately, there was MTV. While she watched a video, her parents got ready to play golf.

"I thought you were going to take a walk," Mr. Naughton said, sticking his head in the door.

Erin shrugged. "I changed my mind."

"Did you see the bulletin board in the lobby?" her mother asked. "It had a whole list of activities."

"For old people," Erin said.

"No. It was specifically for teenagers," her mother said. "Why don't you go take a look?"

Erin shrugged and stared at the music video on the tube.

"I think your mother deserves a reply," Mr. Naughton said.

"Okay," Erin said. "Maybe I'll check it out."

Her parents went off to their golf game, leaving Erin with Bobby. But not for long. A few minutes later Bobby was heading for the door too.

"I'll be in the video room, obliterating cyborgs," he called from the living room. He slammed the door behind him.

The suite was empty. It was silent except for the TV. Erin sat on the bed and watched the screen.

A few minutes later she thought she heard a noise in the living room. It sounded as if someone had quickly opened and closed the door.

"Bobby?" she called.

No one answered.

"Mom? Dad?"

Silence. *That's strange*, Erin thought. She

stood up and went into the living room. At first nothing seemed out of the ordinary. Then she noticed a piece of paper lying on the floor near the door. She picked it up and read: *Your sunglasses are in Room 13.*

Someone from the inn must have left the note for her. Well, good, at least she'd get her glasses back.

A few minutes later, Erin was walking down the hall. A small, thin man approached her. He had long gray hair pulled back into a ponytail, and he was wearing black shorts and a white polo shirt with "New Arcadia" stitched over the pocket.

The man stared at her. It reminded her of the way that waitress Sarah had stared at her earlier. As he came closer Erin felt the same creepy chill she'd felt that morning in the dining room. Erin averted her glance, but not before she read the man's name tag, which said "Sebastian."

After she'd gone another dozen steps, Erin turned back and glanced over her shoulder. To her surprise, Sebastian had stopped and was watching her with a slight smile on his face.

Erin quickened her step. *What a weirdo*, she thought. Jeez, why did her father have to make her come to this dumb inn?

Erin stopped outside Room 13 and knocked. She waited for a few moments, but no one answered. She knocked again. When still no one answered, she figured the people must be out. She'd have to come back for the sunglasses later.

Erin turned away.

"*Erin,*" a voice said.

She stopped and turned back. The hall behind her was empty. *That's strange*, she thought. She was certain she'd heard someone whisper her name. Well, it must have been her imagination.

She started down the hall again.

"*Erin, wait.*"

Erin froze. There was no mistaking it this time. A voice had called to her. Erin looked up and down the hall again, but all she saw were walls, carpeting, and doors.

Maybe I'm going crazy, she thought as she started to take another step.

"*Don't go!*"

Erin stopped again. The whisper had been a little louder and more insistent that time. But there was still no one there.

Unless it was some kind of joke.

"Bobby," she said. "Is that you?"

She waited, but heard nothing. "Bobby?"

"*Here, Erin.*"

It wasn't Bobby's voice. The voice sounded older. And it seemed to be coming from a door to her right. Erin turned. She was standing between Room 15 and Room 13. She took a step toward Room 15.

"*No, over here.*"

Erin stopped and looked at the door to Room 13. She was sure that was where the voice had come from. But why hadn't the person inside answered when she knocked? And how did he know her name? She stared nervously at the brown wooden door and the brass doorknob.

"Who are you?" she asked.

There was no reply.

But she felt something drawing her toward the door. As if it had a mind of its own, her hand grabbed the doorknob and pushed.

The door opened. The room inside was empty except for a single wooden chair and an unmade bed. Her sunglasses were lying on the mattress. Erin quickly picked them up and looked around, puzzled.

"Where are you?" she asked. "Who are you? Come out."

But there was no one in the room. The doors to the closet and bathroom were open, and she could see that no one was inside.

"Isn't anyone in here?" she asked nervously.

Again there was no reply, but suddenly Erin felt a chilly breeze float past her. It felt like a cold draft from an air conditioner, except that there was no air conditioner in the room.

Erin quickly backed out of the room and shut the door.